TRIPLE DARE

Muffin Top Bakery
Book 1

TASHA HART

Description

Love can be bittersweet when you take it nibble by nibble... Just make sure you don't break off more than you can chew.

Bridgid wasn't looking for love when she left her corporate job and returned to her small Texas hometown, but Momma is knocking on Heaven's door, and someone has to manage the family business.

Joel is only there to help with the final arrangements for their small grieving family, and offer counseling to Bridgid in her time of loss. His heart was never on the table.

There's just one problem: ***she's falling in love with him.***

For a girl who has her eyes set on the bright lights and fast pace of the big city, giving your heart to someone who won't leave their small town is definitely a problem. No matter if Joel is a good, decent, honest man that she can picture herself with forever...

Now something's cooking in the kitchen, and it's piping hot—**don't burn your mouth as you sink your teeth into a romance so sweet... It *has* to take place in a bakery.**

bridgid

"Trulia? Hey, sorry to bother you—but I think you need to get here…" I nibbled my lower lip as my voice trails off.

"Why? Is she okay? What's going on?"

"It's bad Tru…" I shake my head, hating the truth. "If you want to say goodbye, then you better hurry…"

"What about Reg? Is she already there?"

"Regina's not here, but I called her. She's on her way. And I'm going to need the help of both of you to settle the estate. I don't know how to do any of this, and it's too much for me. Besides—Reggie's a businesswoman— she'll know more about how to deal with all of this than me."

"I'm on my way, and I'll help with anything you need once I get there. And you know Regina will, too. Just don't get too stressed about it until we arrive. You're not alone in this, Bridgid. I'll be there soon. Love you."

"Love you too." I hang up the phone and let out a small breath of relief. One task done.

My sisters—Regina, Katrina (aka Trulia)—and I have always been very close with our mom. So, when she suddenly had a heart attack, all three of us of course wanted to rush to her side. With me being the only one that still lives in our small Texas town, unfortunately my sisters couldn't be at the hospital right away.

I knew that if she survived the heart attack, it would be a hard recovery—especially when they told me that her diabetes was leading to congestive heart failure. They came out and explained to me that not all conditions that lead to heart failure can be reversed, but that they were doing everything they could. But then when the doctor told me she had no chance of recovery at all?

It broke me.

My world has been turned completely upside down, and we're all still trying to process how this is going to end. Once her doctor told me that she didn't have much longer, Mama insisted on being brought home. She wanted to be comfortable and surrounded by family when her time came.

Her nurse, Raul, has been taking care of her when I'm not home, and today Mama told him that she can feel she doesn't have much time left. I immediately got on the phone with Regina and then Trulia to let them know they needed to get here right away. I just hope they can get here in time—I can't imagine not being able to say goodbye to Mom before she dies.

Before this, I never would have thought it would be me handling everything and planning her funeral—I definitely thought that would have been Regina. And I'm sure Regina will want to take over when she gets here— she's a control freak. But I'm perfectly fine with that. All of this is just too much stress for me—I don't know how to do any of this on top of preparing myself to say goodbye to Mama.

The most stressful thing about this whole process so far has been conversing with the local mortuary. I specifically requested a black undertaker for Mama, but they assigned us a young, white man named Joel. I'm not too happy about it—and on top of that, the funeral director is out of town for some kind of family business—so there's nothing I can really do about it. I guess there are worse things that could go wrong, but it was the *one* request I had.

Anyways, I have an appointment with this Joel tomorrow morning. If only Regina were already here, so she could go for me. I am *not* looking forward to this appointment.

All I want to do is spend all of my time with my mother before she goes. I don't want to miss a single second of the little time she has left.

I know I said we're all close with Mama—but I would definitely say her and I are the closest. We both have the same passion in life—baking. When she was 25 years old, Mama opened her own shop, Muffin Top Bakery. She has run this business successfully all by herself for all of these years, until I recently started taking over for her.

The bakery is her baby—it's like a fourth child to her. She loves it, which is why she wanted to keep it in the family and pass it down to me once she passed. I just never thought it would be so *soon*.

I check on Mama, who turns out to be napping, before going outside and taking a seat under the giant tree in the backyard. Growing up in this house as a kid, I used to come out here practically every day and sit under this tree. I've read so many books, had so many important phone calls and life moments right here. I even come over here still, at age twenty-nine, when I really need to think. It'll be sad when we sell the house, and I won't be able to sit out here anymore.

Of course, it's not some silly tree that I'm actually upset about. It's just too hard to face the truth right now. I just can't do it. My mom has done too much for me, she's made me who I am today. I would be nothing without her. I just can't accept this.

I go inside and quietly crawl into bed with Mama. Curling up next to her like I'm still five, and she isn't dying—I close my eyes and drift off to sleep, pretending like everything's still okay.

joel

My drive to work is quiet and relaxing—something I never could've said back in California. I even have time to stop at a small café near the funeral home for a black coffee before heading in to work.

I've got an extra busy day today. With the funeral director being out of town until further notice, I've had to pick up quite a few more responsibilities than I usually would. It's nothing I can't handle—it's just quite the extra load. I definitely didn't think I would be having this much responsibility so soon—I'm only here on an apprenticeship. Along with that, I also provide grief counseling to all of our clients.

I like to give each and every family that comes through here my undivided attention. The people we work with are going through some of the hardest times in their lives, and they really need us to help make their difficult time just a little easier, if at all possible.

I often get asked if it's depressing to work at a funeral home. The answer is yes, of course. It's always sad to see all these families in their worst moments. Of course, it's hard to meet wonderful people right before they're about to die.

But working in this business—you have to try to separate yourself from the sorrow as much as you can. In fact, you have to. Can you imagine if you went to a funeral home to prepare a service for your loved one, and the staff members are just sobbing along with you? Obviously, we feel the grief that these families are going through—but we have to find a way to remove ourselves from that grief. In other words, you have to be extremely selfless to do this job.

On the harder days, I try to remind myself that I'm helping these people. The family *and* the deceased. They say that funerals are for the living, and while that is true —they really are for the dead. Which is why we pride ourselves in honoring the deceased as best as we possibly can. Everyone deserves to be honored after they die.

Today I have a particularly hard case. I have an appointment with Ms. Bridgid Anne Grant, daughter of Anna Celice Grant. It's always hard for me working with people who have dying mothers, because my own mother passed away a few years ago. It just touches a different part of me when I have cases that are similar to mine.

I pull out the file and look over the details one last time in preparation for our meeting. Ms. Grant is a seventy-two-year-old African American woman, dying of congestive heart failure. She has three adult daughters, one of which I will meet today. Her file includes tons of details about her life, including how she owns her own local bakery. She has lived in Belton, Texas for her entire life—wow.

I only just moved to Belton from Sacramento a little while ago. Truth be told, I thought I was going to despise being here. I'm a Californian at heart, and who would want to leave such a beautiful place?

Surprisingly though, I've really grown to like it here—I might even consider staying. It's very different out here than what I'm used to. I mean, the area is astonishingly beautiful—it really takes your breath away. Just a twenty-minute drive (or less) from the town, I've been able to find beautiful spots where I can sit and stargaze. I'll tell you; you can't do that anywhere in Sacramento.

The parks here are like a different breed, they're extremely nice. Even the local grocery store, HEB, is just *fantastic*. Not to mention the beautiful lakes, and wild animals just about everywhere you look. If you would've told me before I moved here that I would be gushing over grocery stores and lakes—I would have laughed in your face.

I honestly *never* would have thought I would fall in love with small town Texas—especially so fast. But something about this place just feels right to me, almost like a second home. I can envision myself staying here for a long time—much longer than I originally planned.

My thoughts are interrupted by the ring of the front door to the funeral home, signaling that someone has just walked in.

'*Must be Ms. Grant here for her appointment,*' I think as I hurry to the front to greet her. Once the introductions are out of the way, I bring her back to my office to get started.

Chapter Three

bridgid

I AM REALLY NOT LOOKING FORWARD TO THIS appointment. I'm about five minutes away from the funeral home and all I can think about is how I wish Regina were already here, so she could go do this instead.

The main reason I'm so uncomfortable walking into this is because I specifically requested a black undertaker for Mama, and the man I'm about to meet is well, white. I know it's not like a *huge* deal, it's just that I want Mama's funeral to be perfect. I just don't know what I'd do if anything else went wrong right now.

As I try to dismiss these negative thoughts, I pull up to the funeral home and park my truck. I turn off the ignition and grab my purse, but I just can't make myself get out of the car. Walking into this building just makes this all the more real. Mama really is going to die… and although I've known this... I just don't know if I can really face it.

This just doesn't even feel real. How am I here, making funeral arrangements for this woman whom I've loved and looked up to for my entire life. If I had known how little time she had left, I would've spent so much more time with her these past few years. I would've made sure she got to do everything she's ever wanted to do. Now it's too late...

I decide to pull myself together—I can't cry now. If I do, I'm afraid I'll never stop. I *have* to get through this meeting. I take a few deep breaths, and slowly make my way to the front door.

Seconds after I walk in, I'm greeted by Joel Benson, the man who will be taking care of all of Mama's needs.

He introduces himself, shakes my hand, and leads me back to his office. He motions to a small sofa for me to sit on and he takes a seat behind his desk.

"Ms. Grant, I know how stressful all of this planning must be for you when you should really be spending as much time as you can with your mother. So, from now on, you don't have to lift a finger. I am going to take care of everything your mother will need, and I can provide grief counseling for you or any of your family members that might need it."

"Thank you, Mr. Benson. That's really good to know."

"You're absolutely welcome. And please, call me Joel. Now, we just have a few things to get out of the way," he says, pulling out a thick file.

'*A few?*' I think to myself.

"It's important for you to remember while planning the funeral arrangements, that what really matters is your mother. While these small details can get people easily flustered and stressed out—we understand that these things are minute. It's easy to get caught up in wanting everything to be absolutely perfect—but please, let me worry about that."

"Okay," I manage to choke out. I really appreciate how nice Joel is being and how much he seems to really care about this—but right now I just feel completely overwhelmed by grief.

He opens the file and picks out a brochure-type booklet, handing it to me.

"This is a casket catalog. We have many beautiful options for you to choose from, and..."

Joel stops when he notices that I'm crying. I thought I was going to be so strong through this. I thought I could just not let this get to me and do what I had to do for Mama. But staring at this casket catalog, thinking about her lifeless body spending the rest of eternity in one of these… I just can't think about it. I can't. Turns out that I'm nowhere near as strong as I thought I was.

Letting the catalog slide to the floor, I sob into my hands. Suddenly I feel someone sit next to me on the sofa, and when I look over, I see that it's Joel. He places his arm around me and pulls me to him, wrapping me up in his arms.

This small act of kindness only makes me sob harder. I can barely breathe, and my entire body is shaking in his arms. He must think I look crazy, but I'm sure he deals with this all the time, so I just let myself feel this pain.

I don't wanna lose her, I'm not ready. I'm only twenty-nine years old, I'm not ready to lose my mother yet. She won't be at my wedding; she won't meet my children… she won't be here for the most significant years of my life. How the hell am I supposed to cope with that?

I find myself feeling envy for my sisters who are much older and got to spend more time with her than I did. At the same time, I resent them for moving away and leaving Mama with only one of her daughters around.

Who am I going to go to when I have a bad day now? When I have a breakup? What if I run her bakery into the ground? That bakery is the love of her life, and she's put so much work into it. What if I screw it up and the business she has put all of her energy into ends up failing because of me? That would absolutely destroy me.

The more I let the tears flow, the more I spiral. All I can think about are all the worst case scenarios. I can't let my mother down, I just can't. She's my best friend. I can't even imagine myself being successful without her…

joel

When Bridgid's tears subside, I reach over and grab a box of tissues, handing them to her. She thanks me and begins cleaning herself up. I leave my hand on her shoulder for a few minutes longer before removing it.

"Ms. Grant, I really am here to help you with any and everything you could possibly think of. And I know I mentioned this earlier, but I do offer grief counseling. I know sometimes counseling seems a bit silly or one may think they don't need it—but trust me, it really helps. Even if you don't get it from me, you should highly consider getting it from at least someone."

"Thank you, Joel, I might actually take you up on that. Losing Mama is turning out to be a lot harder than I ever could have imagined."

"And that's what I'm here for. And if you do choose to do some grief counseling, I can help you see that this tragedy is not the end of *your* life, too."

I grab the catalogs I had set out on the table in front of us and tuck them away in one of my desk drawers, before returning to my spot next to Bridgid.

"Tell me about your mother." A small smile forms on her face, and she looks up at me.

"Mama is the kindest soul I've ever met in my entire life. She had me when she was forty-three, and so she's always referred to me as her miracle baby. Her and I have always been closer than she was with my two sisters. I think we're just more alike. She has always loved baking; in fact, she's never had a job that didn't involve baking. So, when she was twenty-five, she finally saved up enough to open her own bakery. She didn't even start having kids until after she was successful. When I was born, she had already had that bakery for almost twenty years. And now—she's had it for forty-seven years. I mean, isn't that crazy? A successful business for almost *fifty years*. Not only that, but she has never had any help in managing that place from anyone other than me when I was old enough. And she only hires women. It's an amazing environment. In fact, it's the most popular bakery in the entire county."

The more she talks, the more Bridgid begins to really open up and start venting.

"My two sisters, Regina and Trulia—they're both great and amazing women—but Regina and I have never gotten along. There's always something with us. I'm just worried about how things will be between the two of us when she lands. I don't want to be fighting at a time like this. On top of that, we have to sell Mama's house. I don't want to, but I don't really see another option. The problem is, I wouldn't even know where to begin on how to do that. It's all just too much, not to mention planning the funeral. And I'm sure my sister Reggie will want to take everything over when she gets here, so maybe that will take some weight off of my shoulders—but that still doesn't change the fact that my mother and best friend is *dying...*" A couple more tears escape, and she quickly wipes them away.

I truly feel for this girl. This is definitely going to be one of the hardest cases I've worked on. This woman is so close and so attached to her mother, it really makes me think about me and my own mother before she died. I attempt to comfort her.

"Look, I only just met you—and already I can tell how much you truly love your mother, so my advice is to focus on that and only that. When she dies, your love for her will still be there, and so will her love for you. And try thinking of the bakery as a piece of her. When she's gone, you'll still have that piece of her left. Whenever you miss her, you can go there and continue the work that she loved so much. Maybe it will feel like she's right alongside you. As for your sister, maybe this will be the thing that brings you two together. You're going to need all the support you can get, so this will be the perfect opportunity to lean on her and try to establish that bond that's been missing between the two of you. And you don't have to decide what to do with the house just yet—that can wait for a little while until you have the time and energy to really make a decision and act on it. You don't have to decide *everything* right this instant. All you can do right now is just breathe. Just breathe, and make sure you get the perfect goodbye with your mother that you both deserve." She's silent for a few moments before answering.

"You're right… thank you. I needed that." There's another moment of silence before she continues. "Anyways, we should probably ask Mama what she wants for her funeral."

"No problem, that's what I'm here for. And of course! When would be the most convenient time for you to have me come and speak with her? I'm completely open."

"Tomorrow? I have to pick up my sister from the airport in the morning, so the afternoon would be best."

"Tomorrow afternoon it is then."

"Thank you so much for your time, I'll see you tomorrow."

Once she leaves, I take a seat back at my desk. That was really, really hard. Seeing people like this really takes its toll on me. I have to remind myself constantly that death isn't the only part of life—even if that's what I'm surrounded by all day.

Bridgid seems to be in a really dark place, I just hope that her family can provide her some much needed support once they get here. No one should have to go through this alone. In the meantime, I am going to make sure I do everything I possibly can to make this whole process goes as smoothly as possible for this family.

bridgid

TODAY IS THE DAY THAT TRULIA IS FINALLY ARRIVING. Normally I would be so excited to see her but considering the circumstances—it's a little hard to be excited about anything right now. Honestly, seeing her is going to be really sad. Even though Mama and I are the closest, Trulia has grown to be pretty close with her over the years too.

Trulia's real name is actually Katrina. We used to call her Kat, until one day she came home and announced that she was to be called "Trulia" from now on. From that day on it's been a roller coaster ride with her. Tru is a visual artist living in New York City. She is amazingly talented, and I've always been a little jealous of her spunk. Trulia is the kindest, most compassionate person ever. She's a lot like Mama in that way. The New York scene really is perfect for her, and I'm so proud of how successful she's become.

I arrive at the airport an hour before her flight is supposed to land. I'm very eager to see her. When she finally arrives, we spot each other at the same time. She runs to me, tears already streaming down both of our faces. We hug for a long time, standing in the middle of the airport.

"I'm so glad that you're finally here, this has been hell without you," I say through my tears.

"I know Bee, it's been hell knowing you're here alone and that I'm missing precious time with Mama."

We embrace for a while longer before heading outside to my car. Before we take off, we sit in the car and have a much needed sister talk.

"I can't believe this is even happening Bee… how is this happening?"

"I know… none of this even feels real. I don't even know how to *begin* processing this."

"I feel guilty for moving to New York, I feel like I've neglected you and Mama, and now she's going to die…" Trulia begins sobbing, and I can't help but start tearing up again as well, as I pull her into a hug.

"Don't feel guilty, *please* don't feel guilty. You were just living your life, and there is absolutely nothing wrong with that. Tru, you haven't neglected anyone."

"I just feel like I've wasted all this time not being around her, and now it's too late…"

"But think about all the time you *did* spend with her. Over twenty years, Trulia. That's a long time. Plus, it's not like you haven't been back since you moved, or like you haven't called ad texted her almost every single day."

"Yeah… maybe I'm being a little hard on myself…"

"Trust me, I get it…"

"Bridgid, what are we going to do without her?"

"I try not to think about that…" I say as I start the car and head to my apartment.

"How are the funeral arrangements coming along?"

"Well, I met with that Mr. Joel Benson yesterday to discuss everything. I kind of had a big breakdown right in front of him, and so I didn't actually get anything done. He was really nice to me though, and I no longer worry that he won't be a good fit for Mama. He's supposed to come and meet her this afternoon to discuss her wishes."

"Discuss her wishes… that sounds so morbid. Wow, this is really happening."

"It really is…"

We ride in silence for a few minutes, taking in the fact that we really are planning our own mother's *funeral*. It's a hard thing to process, even for two strong women like us.

"When is Reggie getting here?" Trulia asks after a few minutes.

"Later tonight. The three of us can go get dinner together and catch up and stuff. And you can stay in my guest room while you're here."

"Oh, okay perfect, and who's watching the bakery right now?"

"Annette is there. She's been covering for me a lot since Mama first went to the hospital. She's been a major lifesaver throughout this."

"That's good, that's really good. Hopefully, she can continue covering for you while we sort all of this out."

"Of course, she will, she loved Mama. I know she's super devastated as well, but she understands how much we need her there right now. Anyways, we can hurry up and stash your things at my apartment and then go see Mama before Joel arrives. I want you to be able to see her before he gets there."

"Thank you, Bee. I'm really nervous to see her for some reason…"

"I know… just try to pretend like she isn't sick, like it's any other normal visit…"

She nods somberly, and we drive the rest of the way in silence.

joel

ON MY WAY TO MS. GRANT'S HOUSE, I PREPARE MYSELF for what I'm about to see. It isn't uncommon for me to meet people before they pass away, but usually people come to us after a loved one has already passed. Death is very unexpected. In this case, they knew ahead of time that she was going to die, so it makes sense for me to go and meet her. When I arrive, I expect Bridgid to answer the door, but instead, I'm greeted by a different woman.

"Hi Joel, I'm Trulia," she introduces herself, extending a hand.

"Hi Trulia, pleasure to meet you. You must be the sister Bridgid had to pick up this morning," I say, shaking her hand.

"Yes, that's me! Okay, Mama's in her room so you can just follow me."

As we enter the house, I instantly understand why Bridgid admitted to me that she was having a hard time thinking about letting this house go. It has a certain energy, and charm about it, that I can only assume was established by Ms. Grant over the years. As Trulia leads me through the house, I spot Bridgid coming in through the back door.

"Joel, good afternoon. I can take you to see Mama," she says, relieving Trulia.

We walk down the hall to a closed door. Before we enter, Bridgid turns to me.

"I'm going to go in and let her know that you're here, and then I'll come out and get you. Just remember, she's very weak—so be patient," she warns me. I nod.

Bridgid goes in and shuts the door behind her, leaving me alone in the hall. She's in there for quite some time, so I begin studying the framed photographs that line the walls. There are about ten photos that appear to be of the family. You can really tell how close-knit all of them are. After a few minutes, Bridgid comes back out and stands next to me.

"That one Mama," she says proudly, pointing to a photo of an absolutely *beautiful* young dark-skinned woman.

"Wow... she's breathtaking."

"She really was. Just try to keep that vision of her in your head as we go in, she's ready now," she informs me, leading the way into the room.

Ms. Grant is lying in bed, propped up on some pillows. Bridgid was not exaggerating about her being weak, she looks incredibly frail. I walk over to her bed and take a seat in the chair that Bridgid motions to next to her mother.

"Ms. Grant? It's Joel, nice to meet you."

"Please… call me Mama. I'm Mama," she says.

"Okay, it's nice to meet you Mama. Your daughter has been telling me some absolutely wonderful things about you."

"Did she give you some cupcakes from the bakery? Honey, did you give him some of my delicious cupcakes?"

"I didn't Mama, not yet."

"Oh, please make sure you do, sweetie."

Mama talks very slow and takes many pauses in between sentences. I sit there patiently and wait for her to finish.

"Oh, trust me, after hearing about your amazing bakery —I will hunt these cupcakes down to the ends of the earth if I have to."

This causes Mama to let out a soft laugh. She begins to reach out for my hand, and as soon as I notice, I hold my hand out for her. I don't want her to exert too much energy.

"Tell me about yourself, Joel."

"Well, first and foremost—I'm from Sacramento, California."

"Oh goodness! How did you end up all the way out here?"

"Well, I think it was just time for a change of scenery, but I came for a job opportunity."

"Wow, I've never been to California. In fact, I've barely left Belton throughout my entire life! And I've certainly never been outside of Texas."

"Well, I can definitely see why—this place is absolutely beautiful. You chose the right place."

I can see that Mama isn't ready to talk about her funeral yet, so we continue making small talk. She asks me about my family, I ask her how she got into baking. She even launches into a story about her first ever bakery job. I can sense Bridgid watching us.

After a while longer, Mama finally brings up the funeral.

"I don't want nothin' fancy," she looks at me, her face turning serious. I nod.

I ask her a few questions, but I leave out most of the questions I would normally ask. She tells me her three favorite flowers, and her favorite color. The rest I'll save for the sisters to decide. I don't want to stress this wonderful woman out with the rest of the details.

When that's out of the way, we continue chatting. I want this to feel just like a normal conversation to her, it's easier that way.

"It's very lucky that one of your daughters ended up loving baking as much as you," I say.

"Oh honey, it really is. The first two were total duds, I was starting to get really worried there. To be frank with you, the only reason I even had little Bee over there was in hopes that three was my magic number. Turns out, it was."

"It most certainly was," I say, turning to look at Bridgid, who has a huge smile on her face.

We all laugh, and we talk for a little while longer, until Mama begins nodding off. I look over to Bridgid, who makes sure her mother is comfortable, before leading us out of the room to let her rest.

Chapter Seven

bridgid

I SHUT THE DOOR BEHIND US AND TURN TO JOEL.

"Thank you. Seriously, you were so good with her, and I could tell that she really liked you. We really appreciate it."

"Not a problem at all, your mother is a wonderful woman," he says.

"Okay, let's move into the living room where Trulia should be, and we'll discuss everything."

I lead Joel into the living room, where sure enough, Trulia is waiting for us on the couch.

"Okay, so I didn't want to push your mother too much with too many questions about her funeral—but after speaking with her I got a sense of what kind of service she would like. She doesn't want anything super fancy, but still classy and elegant. With that being said, I already have a few things in mind, so I'll put together a few options for you guys and have you look them over. You guys can decide what you think your mother would like best. After our conversation, I don't think we should bother her anymore about the details of everything. If you think she will like it, then we'll just go with that."

"Sounds good to us. Once Regina gets here, we can all decide together from your options, and let you know which one we agree on," Trulia tells him.

"Agreed, we should wait to decide with Reggie. We can meet you tomorrow if you're free?"

"Of course, I am completely open for tomorrow. Should I meet you guys here or do you three want to come to the funeral home."

Trulia begins to answer but I cut her off.

"Actually, why don't we all meet at the bakery? You can try those cupcakes Mama insisted I give you. Seriously, she's going to keep hounding me about it until I give them to you."

"Ha-ha, I believe you. Meeting at the bakery is good with me, I'm dying to see this wonderful place your mother created anyways."

"Perfect, all right."

Joel reaches out to shake my hand, giving me a warm smile, before turning to Trulia and giving her the same. He begins to walk outside but stops and turns back to us.

"Bridgid, you have my number—this is a challenging time for all of you guys—so if you need anything and I mean *anything*, you just give me a call. I'm available at all hours for grief counseling if any of you need it. Or even if you don't necessarily think you need counseling, I'm always here to listen to you vent. Don't be afraid to ask for help—we all need it at some point."

"Thank you, Joel," I nod at him.

"Yes, thank you very much Mr. Benson."

After he's gone, Trulia and I head back into the house. We both plop back down on the living room couch, visibly exhausted.

"This is a lot, Bee. I'm sorry you've been going at this alone up until now."

"Hey, it was my turn to be the responsible one anyways."

"Are you kidding? You've always been the responsible one, especially when it comes to Mama. Why do you think you've always been her favorite?"

"Hey—that's so not true. Remember when I was with that guy Tony for like a year? Mama and I barely spoke during that time."

"Oh stop, you're exaggerating. She didn't dislike *you*—she disliked your dipshit of a boyfriend."

"Oh whatever," I laugh.

"Anyways, Joel is such a kind man, I'm glad you decided to stick with him. He seems like he really and truly cares about Mama and making this process as easy as possible for us."

"He does, doesn't he? It really makes it a little easier to plan this whole funeral. He was really good with Mama in there—you should've seen them; they were like old friends catching up. Mama really liked him; it was obvious."

"Aw, I'm so glad. I love that he said he didn't push her to give him a bunch of details on what she wants. That was a really smart choice."

"Agreed. Let's just hope Reggie doesn't stir things up when she gets here."

"Ugh, Bridgid please don't fight with her—I don't have the energy to jump in between you two right now."

"I'm not going to fight with her, Tru, I just don't want her showing up and disrupting everything I've already done. You know how she is. If she wanted to be in control, she should've gotten here earlier."

"Yes, I know Bee—but I also know how you are," she says, giving me a look.

"Hey what's that supposed to mean?"

"Oh, come *on*, you've always been extra sensitive when it comes to Reg."

"Yes, but there's a *reason* for that," I say, returning her look.

"Oh whatever, just promise to keep things mature and Zen. We have more important things to worry about."

"I promise. And I also promise that I'm not the one you need to be worrying about."

"If you say so."

Tru has always been the one to have to keep things civilized between Reggie and I—I just hope it doesn't come to that this time. None of us need that.

joel

ONCE WE SAY OUR GOODBYES AND I'M BACK IN MY CAR, I take a moment before driving off. I close my eyes and rest my head against the back of my seat. Talking with Ms. Grant, "Mama", was really eye-opening. It was really hard to see someone so fragile looking but yet so full of life. You can tell that she has accepted that she's going to die, but that she wasn't ready.

One thing is for sure though, those girls were very lucky to have a mother like that. It's just sad that they have to say goodbye to someone so full of love and good energy. I completely feel for what they're going through right now. Especially Bridgid with how close she is to Mama.

After a few minutes, I take off. I head back to the funeral home to start another file on Mama and pick out some options for her service.

I don't usually get this… invested I guess you could say, in my clients. But after meeting Mama, it'll definitely be a little sad picking out some options for her funeral. Even in that short amount of time I spoke with her, I could tell that she is such an amazing woman—I just can't seem to distance myself from this case like I do with all the others. Something about it just makes it harder for me to remove myself from the sadness of this.

When I get back to my office, the first thing I do is start my notes for the day. I write down everything that was said during my conversation with Mama. Usually, I take notes during my chats with people, but I just knew that with Mama I needed to be more present and act as if I was just a friend having a chat.

Once I'm finished taking my notes, I file them away and take a little break before I dive into the rest of my work.

For some reason, I just can't stop thinking about Bridgid. I've already established that this case is hitting me harder than usual, but there's just something about Bridgid in particular that keeps swaying my mind back to her.

It honestly just hurts my heart to see her suffering so much. She keeps her emotions from showing a lot, but you can tell that behind those warm eyes, she is in a lot of pain. Even when she broke down in front of me—I could tell that she was still holding back a lot of her pain. She tries masking it by talking about the other problems she is facing, but I know that she is struggling more than she admits with her mother's impending death.

I know that there's only so much I can do, and that I've already given her the option for grief counseling multiple times now, but I just feel like maybe I need to try harder to get her to open up. I just don't want to see what could happen if she continues to bottle up all of that pain. Some people just need that extra push in order to really accept help.

I definitely see where she's coming from, and I understand the urge to be the strong one for everyone because you feel like that's the right thing to do. Maybe that's why this is hitting me so hard.

I continue contemplating Bridgid and her situation as I begin to put together some options that I know Mama would like, despite my efforts to put her out of my head. I make sure that each option is very reasonably priced, even throwing in some discounts. I want to make this as easy as possible for this family.

Once I'm done, I put them together and print out three packets so that each of the girls can have one to look at. I'm supposed to meet them tomorrow at the bakery, and I'm hoping this meeting can go as smoothly as possible. Sometimes with families deciding these things together, there can be a few bumps in the road. So especially after hearing what Bridgid said about not getting along too well with the third sister—I'm a little worried that there may be some fighting involved in this process.

Once I'm done, I gather all of my things and head home. Once home, instead of making some dinner and settling down to watch my favorite shows, I head straight to bed. For some reason I just have no appetite today, and I kind of just feel like resting.

As I lay in bed, my mind drifts back to Bridgid and her family. Obviously, this isn't my first time dealing with grieving families like this. I've even dealt with cases that were even worse than this one—cases involving murder or suicide. So why is this one hitting me harder than any other? I try telling myself that it's just because I can relate to it because of my own experience with grief, but I know that's not entirely why. I just can't seem to put my finger on it.

Every single family I deal with is hard. Seeing so much pain and loss really does take a toll on you. No matter how much you prepare yourself and how many times you do it, it never gets easier. Sometimes it even gets harder as time goes on. Maybe that's why this is affecting me so much. Maybe I've just hit a breaking point in my career… maybe I'm finally cracking.

I end up staying awake for hours despite how exhausted I am. For a while I just brainstorm ways that I can make this easier for the Grant family. But what I'm mostly thinking about is how to help Bridgid. Something about that girl just won't leave me.

Chapter Nine

bridgid

THE DRIVE TO THE AIRPORT TO PICK UP REGGIE IS completely silent. I think both Trulia and I are just exhausted from this day already. Even though the meeting with Joel went well, it's still very stressful for us.

When Mama woke up from her nap earlier, we tried to get her to have a bite to eat, but she said she was too tired, and she ended up falling back asleep. It was a little worrying because she didn't even want some baked goods from the bakery—and I've never seen Mama turn down baked goods before—especially her own. Even though her nurse, Raul is there with her, it's just hard to leave her.

When we arrive at the airport, we head to the waiting area outside of the gate Regina is supposed to land at. No matter how much I tell myself that things with Reg will be fine—that we'll all be focused on what's important

—Mama, I'm still just extremely stressed out by her arrival.

Reggie and I haven't actually gotten along since I was about four, so I barely even remember it. Apparently, we were inseparable up until that point. Our personalities are just so polar opposite that I don't know how we're even related to each other sometimes.

She's always been very controlling over everyone and everything. She wants things her way or no way. I, on the other hand, am the complete opposite. While I of course have my preferences, I have always been a very chill and laid-back person. I'm more go with the flow, while Regina feels the need to control the flow.

Not only that, but Regina feels the need to bulldoze over people. Meaning if someone has an idea or wants something a certain way, she completely disregards them and their feelings and forces things to be the way *she* wants them instead. Basically, she's just incredibly insensitive. But obviously I still love her—after all she is still my sister.

"Hey, remember that year that Reggie didn't like the homecoming theme everyone picked at school, so she held rallies to change it until they finally gave in?" Trulia asks.

Ugh, case in point. I groan out loud.

A couple minutes later, the plane lands and people begin deboarding. Finally, we spot Regina.

"Oh my god we are getting food like *now*—I'm fucking starving," Regina says as she joins us.

"Really? That's how you greet us?" I ask. Regina rolls her eyes.

"Why hello Bridgid, it's nice to see you," her voice drips with sarcasm.

Trulia shoots me a look and pulls Reggie in for a hug.

"Don't worry, we're starving too. We've barely eaten all day," she says.

We grab Reggie's bags and head to the car. Once everyone is ready to go, I turn to my sisters.

"So, where are we eating Regina?"

"Oh you're going to let me choose?"

"What are you talking about? You literally always choose everything."

"Guys, please don't start. We're not here to fight. Let's just go get Italian. Who fucking cares where we eat," Trulia jumps in.

Once again, we ride in silence. I really didn't mean to pick a fight with Reggie so soon, I guess I just can't help myself. I've got a lot of anger built up in me and Regina just happens to be the only one I can take any of that out on.

We arrive at the restaurant and get seated right away. Reggie makes a point not to sit next to me. After the waiter takes our order, she starts discussing her plans.

"So, I've arranged for a rental car to have during my stay to make things easier."

"Okay, well tomorrow we have an appointment at the bakery with the man from the funeral home, Joel. He's going to show us the options he chose for Mama's service," Trulia informs her.

"Okay, so then I'll just have the rental car pick me up from the bakery after the appointment. You guys can drop me off and pick me up from my hotel room until then."

"You didn't have to get a hotel room," I tell her, an attempt to be nice.

"Too late now," she says, avoiding eye contact.

"Okay guys, we have to make a pact tonight," Trulia states. Without waiting for our responses, she continues on. "This is obviously an extremely tough time. We're all under a lot of stress on top of grieving Mama. And the only people we truly have is each other. So, we need to make a pact that during this time, we will only show each other love and kindness. Which means absolutely *no fighting*. Does this sound fair to you guys?"

"Absolutely," Regina says. They both turn to me.

"Yes. No fighting." I state. Our food arrives just then, saving us from any further comments that might have been made.

"Man, this is delicious," Trulia says after a couple bites of her lasagna, tomato sauce all over her mouth. We all laugh, and for just a moment it feels like we're just three sisters hanging out, instead of three sisters planning their mother's funeral.

The rest of our dinner goes well. We fill Reggie in on what's been going on with Mama and convince her that she doesn't need to go see her tonight because she'll still be sleeping. We agree to go see her tomorrow after our appointment with Joel.

I drop Regina off at her hotel room, and Tru and I head back to my apartment.

"You did pretty good tonight," she says.

"Ha! You're joking right? That was a horrible start."

"Yeah it was, I was just trying to be nice."

I throw my pillow at her and we laugh.

"Tomorrows going to be really hard," Trulia sighs.

"That's the understatement of the year. But it won't be the hardest day to come."

"Yeah…"

"Hey why don't you sleep in here tonight? It's been a while since we had a good old-fashioned Twin sleepover, and I could use the company," I offer. Her face lights up. Tru and I aren't *actual* twins, of course, but we've always referred to ourselves as such because of how close we are.

"That's a great idea, I'll go get changed into my pajamas."

For the rest of the night, Tru and I watch our favorite movie together and reminisce over our childhood with Mama. It's a really good bonding moment, and it feels good to not be completely alone for once.

joel

I wake up even more tired than I was when I went to bed—I barely got any sleep last night. I make myself some coffee—black with no sugar—and once I'm ready I gather my things. Even though I already put together options for the girls to choose from, I look them over one last time before I leave for my meeting. I just hope they like one of them. I don't want this to be stressful for them.

Turns out the Muffin Top Bakery is closer to my house than I thought it was. How have I never spotted it before? The parking lot is empty except for one car, which I'm sure is Bridgid's. I'm a little early, but I grab my papers and head in anyways. The door is locked, but Bridgid spots me right away and lets me in.

"Okay, Joel you've already met my sister Trulia," Trulia nods and waves. "But you haven't met Regina yet.

Regina, this is Joel." Regina looks a bit skeptical when she sees me, but she gets up to shake my hand.

"Hi Joel, nice to meet you."

"Nice to meet you as well, Regina."

"Now, before we get to business—I'm going to make you a cup of coffee, and while I do that you can pick whatever you'd like to eat. We have so many delicious breakfast options, and I'll pack you some cupcakes to go," Bridgid says, handing me a small menu to look at.

"Wow, thank you," I accept, even though I already had a cup of coffee before coming here.

I order a strawberry strudel, and Bridgid brings me a small cup of caramel colored coffee. I take a sip, and immediately look to Bridgid.

"Oh my god—I've never had coffee that wasn't completely black before… this is amazing."

"Ew, you don't put *anything* in your coffee?" Trulia asks.

"Never. But now that I know how good it is like this, I don't think I can ever drink it my way again." Bridgid and Trulia chuckle. Regina looks at her phone, seemingly annoyed. I decide it's time to get to work.

"Okay, so I made you each a small packet to look through with a few different options to choose from," I inform them, handing them each a packet. "From my discussion with Mama, I think any of these will make her very happy."

"*Very happy?* You think *this* will make her happy? It's her fucking funeral—" Regina starts, only to be cut off by Trulia.

"Reggie—be nice. You know what he meant. Just look through the options, don't be rude."

My face is blood red, and I feel humiliated.

'*I should have worded that differently, I should have been more sensitive,*' I think to myself.

After a few minutes, Trulia speaks again.

"I think all of these are great, but the second one is perfect for Mama."

"I agree, the second one is exactly what she would have chosen," Bridgid agrees.

"That one was my favorite too. Based off of what she told me, I think that option will really suit her."

"You guys aren't serious…" Regina says, looking back and forth between her sisters.

"What?" They both ask.

"None of these options are even *remotely* close to what I envisioned for Mama. I'm sorry, but these are just not going to do. I think we can pick something much better than *this*," Regina says, gesturing to the packet. She slides it back across the table to me and begins telling us what she has in mind.

"While that sounds very lovely, none of that is in the price range I was given," I inform her.

"Reggie, there's nothing wrong with what he picked out. Why don't you like these?"

"You can't be serious right now. I will not allow Mama to be disgraced like this. She deserves a proper funeral, not whatever the hell that was."

"Reggie now you're just being plain mean."

"I'm being mean? Oh, *I'm* sorry. I just want my *mother* to have a proper *funeral*."

"So, do we." Bridgid states, noticeably upset.

This is exactly what I was worried was going to happen. I feel so awkward and I can't even make myself say anything. I thought I had put together some wonderful options, and this girl is just completely offended by them. I have no idea what to do… at this very moment, I wish I could just disappear.

bridgid

I KNOW I PROMISED TRULIA YESTERDAY THAT THERE would be no more fighting—but even she has to admit that Regina is being a complete bitch right now for no reason.

"Reggie—Joel already spoke to Mama yesterday. I was there. She told him what she wanted, and he took that and put this together for us. Need I remind you that you weren't here for any of this?"

"Okay that's it. You don't have to keep rubbing that in my face. I got here as fast as I could. I know *you* don't have a life—but I *do*, so it wasn't that easy for me to drop everything and run here."

"She's your *mother* Regina. What could possibly be more important?"

"Katrina got here the same exact day that I did—and yet I don't see you yelling at her!"

"Her name is *Trulia* and I'm not yelling at you for when you got here, I'm yelling at you for being a *bitch*."

"How am I being a bitch? I'm only trying to make sure that Mama gets the service that she deserves."

"And we're trying to give Mama the service that she *asked for*, what don't you understand about that? Seriously— what is it that you aren't getting?"

"Mama's too nice to say what she really wants—but trust me—*that* shit is not what she wants."

"Right—because you know everything, right?"

"I don't know everything, but I *do* know what's *best*."

"What makes you *so* sure of that?"

"Bridgid, I'm older than you. I've known Mama the longest."

"Have you? Because I would say that all these years that you've been gone kind of says the opposite. You may be older, but that doesn't mean jack shit. Who has been the one by Mama's side every single day for years on end? Who was the one that stayed with her in the hospital? Who's been the one handling everything? Because I know for damn sure that that was *not* you."

"Guys *stop* yelling at each other. Reggie, you kind of *are* being a bitch. Bridgid has been the one dealing with all of this, and Joel has been so kind to all of us, especially Mama. You're being extremely disrespectful to that right now," Trulia jumps in.

"Honestly, Katrina? I really don't care what *you* have to say right now."

"It's Trulia. My name is Trulia. And what the hell is that supposed to mean?"

"You know exactly what it means. Just please stop acting like you're the golden child."

"I'm not acting like anything; I'm just trying to get you two to stop fighting for one second. Clearly you can't even be mature enough to stop this bullshit when our own mother is *dying*."

"Tru, it's okay. You don't have to get involved in this. And please remember that it was Regina who started this. Everything was fine until she started yelling at everyone and trying to force thing to go her way, as usual."

"Oh, Bridgid just stop. Seriously, just stop. All I was trying to do was make sure that Mama was being honored the way that she deserves to be. You don't have to make me out to be such a bad person all the time."

"Regina—I don't have to make you out to be anything— you don't hide it—everyone can see it *very* clearly."

"Honestly, I don't care what anyone thinks of me. I told the man what I want the funeral to look like, and that's that. If he won't do it, I'll find someone else who will. Matter of fact, I'll just find someone else regardless."

"No, no you won't. You can't always have everything your way. I'm sorry but it just isn't going to happen this time. I'm not going to let you bulldoze over all of us like you always do. Not this time. This is *Mama's* funeral—not yours. So, it will look how *she* wants it to look. God, I can't believe I even have to say this to you. It's like trying to teach a five year old manners."

"I'm sorry Reggie, but she's right," Trulia jumps in again, "Mama wants it this way, and it's up to her—not you."

"Oh well of *course* you're taking her side—you *always* take her side. When will this end?" Regina shouts, tears streaming down her cheeks.

"It'll end when you stop being a bitch, Regina." I state, refusing to feel sorry for her just because she breaks out the tears.

"You know what—I'm not doing this. My car is here, I'm leaving," Regina says, storming out in tears.

I cannot believe that just happened. I don't feel bad for her one bit. This is exactly what she always does—she acts like a bitch and tries to control everything, and the *second* that anyone stands up to her, she plays the innocent act and starts crying. I'm not falling for it this time, and I hope Tru doesn't either. I'm done with this.

The fact that Reggie couldn't even be mature enough to drop her usual bullshit—considering the circumstances right now—really says a lot to me about her character.

I look over at Joel, who's been completely silent since Regina started complaining. He's staring down at his strawberry strudel, face red, looking extremely uncomfortable. I feel bad that he just had to witness that, and I'm angry at Reg for forcing him to, after everything he has already done for this family. But of course, she doesn't care about that, she only cares about herself.

I have no idea how I'm going to get through the upcoming weeks, or however long Regina is going to be in town for. I shake my head and take a sip of my coffee. This was not how today was supposed to go.

joel

THIS MEETING HAS DONE A FULL ONE-EIGHTY, AND FOR the past twenty minutes they've all been arguing. I'm not sure if this is my fault, or if this is just how Regina always is—but I can't help but feel a little responsible. I know I only just met the girl, but I imagine that having some stranger walk in and tell you what your own mother wants, must have been a little frustrating.

Finally, Regina storms out of the bakery, and I can't help but feel relieved. I let out the breath I'd been holding in. This whole situation has been so uncomfortable and awkward, I just want this to be over with already. I've never been in a situation quite like this before, and so I have no idea what to do.

The entire time the three of them were practically screaming at each other, I just stared at my uneaten strudel. I didn't want to get in the middle of their family matter, so I figured the best thing to do was act invisible. Although, at times it was a little hard to stop myself from speaking up, considering how rude that girl was.

I finally will myself to look up just as Trulia grabs her purse and stands up.

"I'm going to go after her and try to calm her down. That was obviously horrible—but she's still our sister. I have to go after her. I'm sorry. I'll call you later or get a ride back to your apartment, Bee. And Joel—I am so *so* sorry. I will find a way to make this up to you." With that, she runs outside to catch up with Regina.

I look to Bridgid, who avoids eye contact. She puts her head down on the table for a few moments before finally looking up at me, letting out a sigh.

"Joel, I'm really sorry. This is not how today was supposed to go—at all. I can't believe you just had to sit through that. That must have been so uncomfortable for you."

We sit in silence for a little bit before I muster up an answer. I don't really know how to respond to that, because to be honest—I'm still in complete shock about what just happened, and I'm not really sure what my place here is right now. I should probably just grab my stuff and leave, giving her some space—but that just doesn't feel right. I decide to stay and try to help her out if she wants me to.

"Look, don't feel bad. That wasn't your fault. In fact, that wasn't anyone's fault. I've learned that some people become their worst selves when they're grieving because they don't know how to cope with all of their emotions. I think your sister is just channeling all of her anger right now so that she doesn't have to feel the sorrow that's inside of her."

When she doesn't say anything, I continue.

"Look, why don't you let me close up the bakery early for you? I'm sure you don't really feel up to dealing with any customers right now."

"Actually, can you? That would be so great, thank you," she says, forcing a smile.

"Of course, it's no problem," I nod and get up to go lock the door and flip the open sign to closed. I go behind the counter and just start cleaning anything that looks like it needs to be cleaned. I don't want her to have to deal with any of this, after the morning she just had. Once everything looks up to snuff, I grab some napkins, and sit back down next to Bridgid.

I hand her the napkins, and after thanking me she wipes away a few tears. Suddenly she looks out the window, as if she just realized it was there.

"Let's go to my office where there aren't any windows—I don't want any customers to happen on by and see me having a mental breakdown," she laughs, trying to make light of the situation.

"Good idea."

She leads me back to her office and plops down on a loveseat in the corner. The minute she sits down, she begins sobbing. I rush over to her, sitting down and putting an arm around her. For a long time, she just cries and cries. All I can do is just hold her and try to stop myself from joining in on the crying.

Seeing anyone like this is tough—but seeing Bridgid like this? My heart feels like it's breaking the longer she sobs into my chest. A few tears escape my eyes, and I wipe them away quickly, not wanting her to see. I caress her hair, trying to calm her down a bit. I wish there were more—or *something* that I could do to erase all of the pain from this girls' mind. She doesn't deserve this.

bridgid

As I cry, it feels as if every single emotion I've ever held in is coming out. I can't even think, all I can do is just feel this pain. Joel is nice enough to hold me as I cry. Of course, he is—Joel is the nicest man I've met throughout my entire life.

I cry for Mama, who's dying, I cry for Regina, who clearly needs help. I cry for Trulia, who always has to clean up our messes—who always gets stuck in the middle of our fights. I cry for myself, because everything is just too overwhelming for me right now.

Joel rubs my back and massages my neck, trying to comfort me. Eventually the tears slowly begin to subside. Joel is so calm and patient with me as I deal with these emotions, and I feel so unbelievably grateful for him.

After a while, I sit up and look at Joel. He looks tired, and sad.

"How do you do this?" I ask.

"Do what?"

"How do you continue to do this job, after seeing so much pain and grief all the time? I mean, how does it not get to you?"

The initial look on his face is shock, but then he seems to pause and think for a moment before answering.

"You know—the loss of a loved one is a terrible time in anyone's lives—no matter how prepared you think you are for it. When we lose someone we love—we feel lost, we feel alone. And in this job—well, it's my job to help those people grieve properly. It's my job to try to make the process go by as smoothly as it possibly could go. Now, of course it doesn't always work out that way— because losing people will never be easy. But it's my job to at least try. Someone has to…"

He sounds so wise; it makes me wonder how he got this way.

"I mean, trust me—I've definitely thought about doing other work. Something less stressful, something more upbeat—but the fact of the matter is—this is where I belong. This is my calling, and I'm grateful that I was gifted with the strength to do this. And to answer your question—it does get to me. But I just have to remind myself that the people I'm helping feel even worse than I do, and so they need me to remain neutral for them."

"How did you know that this was what you wanted to do?"

"Actually… I lost my own mother a while back. It was the worst time in my life—the absolute worst. I thought I was going to break—I thought I would never be able to come back from that. But somehow, I did. And you know who helped me do that? The grief counselor that was working with my family. He saved me—quite literally. And after that, I decided that I wanted to save people the same way he did me. Besides, I can't think of anything more fulfilling than being there for the bereaved."

I stare at him for a moment before responding. I never would have guessed that this man sitting in front of me had gone through the very same thing I'm going through right now—he seems so strong. And the fact that he has been able to sit here and help me while I'm crying over my dead mother—when he was in my very position at one point? That's truly amazing. It starts to make sense the more I think about it—in order to help people get through something—it helps if you've been through it yourself.

"That's actually really beautiful, Joel. I didn't know you'd been through that…"

"Yeah, well it's not my job to confide in you—it's my job to get you to confide in me."

"Well, clearly you do your job very well," I laugh, gesturing to my wad of tissues.

"Ha-ha, well what happened out there kind of makes me think I'm doing anything *but* helping."

"Hey, that is *not* true. As much as that had nothing to do with me—it had nothing to do with you. I promise. You put together wonderful options for us that were exactly what Mama wanted and asked you for—Regina is just a spoiled brat who will kick and scream any time she doesn't get her way. I'm afraid there's nothing that can really be done about that."

"Do you think that she would benefit from some grief counseling herself?"

"Honestly? I think Reggie's problems go back way further than this. Believe it or not—she's kind of always been like this."

He nods, the thoughtful look returning to his face.

"I love that you're always trying to figure out how you can help everyone," I tell him.

"Well, I wouldn't be doing my job if I didn't try to do that," he says, blushing.

'*Always so humble,*' I think.

Sitting here talking with Joel like this feels good. For a few minutes, I actually forgot about Regina and the whole fight. He's good like that.

I stare at him, finally noticing how handsome he is. His dirty blond hair that seems to always fall perfectly in place at any given moment. His big, deep blue eyes… how have I not noticed this until now?

This is the humblest, most kind, compassionate, and wise man I think I have ever met. And he has certainly shown me more kindness and patience than anyone ever has before. At this moment, all I can think about is how amazing this man is…

Next thing I know, I'm leaning in towards him. I place my hand on his thigh, and my other hand on the side of his face. We look each other in the eyes for a moment, before I move my hand to the back of his neck and pull him to my lips.

The moment we touch, I forget about everything. Everything. We move our lips in sync, becoming more urgent by the second. I want more. I need more. His hand slips around my waist, squeezing my skin. Our lips continue working together, and I can't help but notice how right this feels.

Suddenly, he starts to pull away. He looks at me, an odd, unreadable expression on his face. I look at him in confusion—why would he pull away? I begin to move back in, but he stops me.

joel

"Bridgid—I'm not so sure that this is a good idea…"

It's not that I'm not attracted to her—of course I am, who wouldn't be? It's just that this is my client, who is going through a very rough time right now. And I don't want our heightened emotions to get the best of us in this very challenging time for her. I don't want either of us to end up getting hurt by whatever seems to be happening right now.

She smiles softly at me, an almost knowing smile. She lifts her hand and caresses my cheek ever so gently, like she's admiring me. Tingles run up my spine. She slowly hooks her hand around the back of my neck again and pulls me closer, eyes never straying from mine. Screw it.

I meet her halfway and our lips collide again. It feels even better than the first time, probably because this time I have thrown all rationalities out the window. The longer we kiss, the harder I can feel myself getting. I want her so bad.

She moves into my lap, fiercely grinding against me. I let a moan escape my body, which she takes as an invitation. She pulls my shirt off, running her hands along my body. Her touch is like fire in my veins. There is a sense of urgency between us.

I want this girl so bad—I want to taste her, I want to feel myself inside of her… I want to touch every part of her. I pull her shirt off, revealing her breasts. Grabbing her by the waist, I switch positions with her, so that she's no longer in my lap. I take one of her breasts in my hand and bring my mouth to her nipple while looking up into her eyes. I want to see the look of pleasure on her face when I touch her.

As I swirl my tongue around her nipple, taking it into my mouth and nibbling at it with my teeth, I use my free hand to rub her other nipple in between my fingers. I'm driving her crazy, I can tell. She runs her hands through my hair, grabbing tufts of it and pushing my head even closer to her.

I nip and bite at her, sucking until her nipples are raw. My fingers trail down the rest of her body, my mouth following. When I get to her hips, I rip off her jeans, panties along with them, and begin kissing her softly. I kiss and lick around her lips and around her opening— but not quite touching the parts she wants me to touch the most. She groans like she's in pain, but I know she's enjoying my teasing.

When I finally think she's had enough, I decide to take it one step further. I hover my tongue over her clit, *almost* touching it, and I lick the air above it. And then I give her what she wants.

I take her clit in my mouth, causing her to cry out while her back arches. This is exactly why I teased her, because when I finally give her what she wants, it feels even better.

I flick my tongue against her clit, slowly increasing the speed. As I do this, I massage around her opening with my fingers before inserting one. Then two. Then three. The double stimulation drives her wild, and I can feel her body quivering.

I flick my tongue at the top of her clit as fast as I can while massaging my fingers inside of her against her g-spot until her back arches, and she's practically screaming with pleasure as she comes.

I lick her clean before moving back onto the couch, taking a seat next to her. She's completely out of breath as she gets back into my lap and rests her head on my shoulder until her breathing goes back to normal.

She begins to kiss my neck, my earlobes, and then my lips, tasting herself. Kissing her now, after what we just did, is more intimate than before. We feel closer. I have to admit, seeing her in such bliss made me feel something I've never felt before. All I want to do is make her come again. And I will.

I begin to unbuckle my pants; except she pushes my hands away and does it for me. Bridgid already has a way of touching the most sensitive parts of my mind like no one else can, I wonder if she can do the same to my body too.

She slips the rest of my clothes off and begins grinding her wet clit along my length. This feels so amazing, and all I want right now is to be inside of her. I want to hear her scream again and come at the same time as her…

bridgid

JUST AS HE'S ABOUT TO ENTER ME, MY PHONE RINGS. FOR a second, I think I've imagined it, but there it is, loud and clear. Joel and I spring apart, and we've clearly both snapped out of whatever spell we were just under.

I run over to my desk and grab my phone. It's Trulia.

"I have to answer this—it's Tru, it could be about Mama," I inform him. He nods, while getting up and scrambling to put his clothes back on. Standing there naked, I answer the phone.

"Is everything okay?" I ask. Any phone call from my sisters or Mama's nurse could be news about Mama's condition, and so it terrifies me every time. I don't want to hear that she died over the phone, and worst of all— without me there…

"Everything is fine. Sorry I didn't mean to worry you, I texted you, but you weren't responding. Listen, I'm here with Regina and I managed to get her to calm down. Everything's okay now, and hear me out—I think we should all have dinner tonight."

I cannot believe this.

"Are you fucking kidding me? After the way she spoke to me—and you—earlier, you seriously want me to sit down and have dinner with her now? You must be joking."

"No, Bridgid—I'm not joking. This is the time for you to be the bigger person."

"I am *always* the bigger person when it comes to Reggie, and you know that. I can't do it anymore. I just can't. Especially not with everything going on."

"Everything going on is exactly the reason that you need to be the bigger person. What's one more time? Come on Bee, how many more dinners do we have left with Mama?"

She's right. We don't know how many more days we'll even have with Mama, and we have to make the most out of each day we do have left—regardless of what's going on between the three of us.

"Fine. I'll be there. But I'm coming for Mama—not Regina," I state, hanging up.

Joel is awkwardly sitting on the couch, avoiding eye contact. I grab my clothes and begin to get dressed, occasionally glancing over at him. Damn, that orgasm was fucking amazing… I really fucking needed that. But that doesn't make this any less awkward. I'm not really sure where to go from here.

Once I get dressed, I take a seat next to him. We look at each other and smile, but the tension is high.

"Look, Joel—I don't regret what just happened… at all. That was amazing. But I honestly don't know what anything in my life means right now. I'm in such an odd place…"

"I don't regret it either…um, I've never been in this situation before with a client, but you don't have to stress about it. I completely understand, you're going through a lot. This won't happen again."

'Whew, glad that's over with,' I think.

Joel gets up and begins to head for the door.

"Hey, can you leave one of those packets you made? I know Regina was a bitch earlier—but we'll agree on one of your options. We'll think about it and I'll let you know what we decide."

"Okay, sounds good!"

"Come by the bakery some time!" I shout as he heads out of my office.

Well, that was cringe worthy…

Once Joel leaves, I clean up my office and head back to my apartment to change before dinner. Today was an eventful one, to say the least. What started out as a simple meeting about funeral arrangements, turned into a massive fight—leading to sex in my office. What is my life?

After I shower and change, I plop down in bed. I still have a couple hours before I need to be at Mama's for dinner. I think about my encounter with Joel. Why did Trulia have to call me right then? My body shudders thinking about what would've happened if we hadn't gotten interrupted. I start to get turned on again.

I need to stop. Whatever happened with Joel earlier, can *never* happen again. I'm not in the right head space for anything right now—not even booty calls. If we continue this, someone is definitely going to end up hurt—and I do *not* want to be the one to hurt him. Joel has been so amazing to me and my family—he doesn't deserve that.

But ugh, I can't stop thinking about the way his tongue felt on my body. How am I just supposed to forget that? How could anyone? I feel like a horrible person… my mom is dying, and I'm sitting here thinking about sex.

I try taking a nap, so I can clear my mind a little before dinner, but I just can't stop thinking about today's events. How am I going to get through a whole dinner with

Regina without arguing after what happened earlier? Or better yet—how am I going to get through a whole dinner without thinking about what Joel would have felt like inside of me?

I shake my head, grab my purse, and head to Mama's house. I turn my music up high the whole way there as to distract myself. I just want to have a good night with Mama—for Mama. This will be the first time all four of us have had a meal together in a long time. That makes me really sad.

When I arrive, they're almost done cooking. I jump in and help with whatever I can, before going to check on Mama. Turns out she's taking a nap, so that she can have as much energy as possible for our dinner. Regina and I don't speak or even make eye contact with each other.

joel

AFTER LEAVING HER OFFICE, I HEAD TO THE BATHROOM to wash what's left of her off of my face. Once I'm all cleaned up, I leave Bridgid one of the packets, as requested, and head out. I don't even know what to think about what just happened. I don't even know where to begin.

Honestly, I think Bridgid is fucking amazing. Like truly—I've never met a girl quite like her. Obviously, the situation is awkward and unfortunate—but Bridgid is special. I can't help but feel like there's something there that I can't just ignore.

I drive back to the office and go about the rest of my day in a complete daze. I barely even remember my conference call with the funeral director. Since he's still out of town, I have to call him every other day to catch him up on things. For all I know, I told him I had sex with one of my clients today. Yeah, no—he definitely would have fired me if I did that.

After I finish work, I stop at a local diner for some grub. I order some chicken noodle soup, and dive in. My mother used to always make me this whenever I was having a day or needed to think. She called it her "brain food". She said it would help clear my head. Here's to hoping she was right because I really need that right now.

When I've finished my soup, I pay my bill and head home. I'm driving for about thirty minutes before I realize I have completely passed my exit to go home and I've driven about fifteen minutes out of the way. Instead of getting flustered, I realize that maybe this is exactly what I need to clear my head. I turn down an old country road and drive until I'm far enough from all the city lights and pollution to see the stars.

I pull over to the side of the road and sit on the hood of my car. For a long while I just stare at nothing. Then I start thinking about Bridgid. I think about how strong and beautiful she is, and how I've been forcing myself not to notice those things because she's my client. This is not the type of job where it's exactly acceptable to fall for your clients…

I think about her reaction when I told her about my mom. I've never, *ever* told a client about my mother before. I *always* keep my personal life completely separate. Like I told Bridgid—my job isn't to confide in them, it's to get them to confide in me.

I wonder what my mom would think of me if she saw me now. Would she be proud of me? Would she be disappointed in me for my latest involvement with Bridgid? I try to think of what she would say to me right now if I was venting to her. She would probably tell me to do whatever feels right, and that I should trust myself. But what if I'm telling myself two different things? Which part am I supposed to trust then?

I take out my phone, pulling up Bridgid's contact. It's pretty late, she's probably back home from the dinner already… should I call her? I debate this for several minutes before putting my phone back in my pocket. She made it very clear earlier that she didn't want anything to happen again—and calling her regarding anything other than Mama might be disrespecting that.

I lay back and stare at the stars, reciting to myself all the reasons that being with Bridgid would be a bad idea. Well, for starters—she's my client. Being romantic with the person who is paying me is just messy and inappropriate by any standards.

Number two—she's grieving—and she's only at the beginning of this process. She still has a long way to go in her grief—she can't possibly add a new person into her life so soon after losing someone. It would be too much for her, and I don't want to take advantage of her vulnerable state. I think back to when I first lost my own mother—I most certainly was not in any place to be welcoming new relationships into my life, especially not romantic ones.

But does any of that matter if I'm falling for her? Or if she happens to be falling for me? Love is the most important thing in life, and if I have a chance to have it —who am I to turn that down?

This is too much to think about, and yet I can't turn my mind off.

'*So much for that chicken noodle soup Mom,*' I think to myself.

After another hour, I get back in my car and head home. It's a long drive, and once I'm finally home I am beyond exhausted. I take a quick shower and jump in bed.

Considering how exhausted I am, I figure I'll fall asleep right away. But instead, my mind lingers back to Bridgid… again. I can't stop thinking about how amazing it was with her earlier. How right it felt to have her lips pressed against mine. How our bodies were so in sync and seemed to know exactly what the other wanted and needed.

I resent the phone call that interrupted what I'm sure would have been an amazing orgasm, and I find myself fantasizing about what would have happened had we not been interrupted. How it would have felt to be inside of her…

I get back up, splash some water on my face, and get back in bed. I will myself to stop thinking about her—and eventually, I drift off.

Chapter Seventeen

bridgid

Once all the food is done and Raul has seated Mama nice and comfy, we load up our plates and join her in her room. We were all going to eat in the dining room because Mama loves it in there so much—she spent years decorating it to her liking—but she was just too tired and so it's best that she stays in bed.

Reggie and Tru made a delicious meal—Cajun fried chicken, Mama's recipe of buttery mashed potatoes, and a ton of veggies on the side. A classic Southern dinner.

Dinner starts off dead quiet. Neither me nor my sisters want to be the first one to talk. It's incredibly awkward, considering that the last time all three of us were in a room together was the screaming match this morning.

None of us want to bring up this morning's events because we don't want to risk upsetting Mama, and she hates when any of us fight. Besides, she shouldn't have to worry about any of that right now—her funeral arrangements *or* her daughters not getting along. We want her last days to be as peaceful as possible. Although I'm sure she can tell that something's going on with us— she's smart like that.

Eventually, Mama breaks the silence.

"You know, that Joel sure is handsome…" she blurts out.

All three of us burst out laughing.

"Mama!" I shout, face burning up.

"What? He is! I'm just simply telling it like it is. If I were as young as you girls, I'd jump right on that man as soon as the opportunity presented itself." Oh Mama, if only you knew…

We burst out laughing again. This is just like Mama to say something like this, and it makes me smile seeing a bit of her personality shining through even in the face of her illness. This woman really has no filter. I can't believe she's going to be gone soon… I look over at my sisters, who must be thinking the exact same thing, because both of them have tears streaming down their faces. Seeing this triggers an even deeper sadness in me, and I start crying too.

"Oh Mama, we're going to miss you so much…" Trulia says, putting down her plate and cuddling up next to

Mama.

I put my plate aside and join her on the opposite side. Regina lays at the foot of the bed.

"I know… I know y'all will—but listen here. Don't go being too sad for too long, okay? I've lived a long seventy-two years, and I got to do everything I ever dreamed of—including being a mother to my three *beautiful* daughters. Even if I had regrets, they don't matter one bit now," Mama pauses to take a breath.

"Please be kind to one another. I know how y'all fight—and I don't like it one bit, never did. No matter who you meet out in that world, the most important people are already in this very room. As long as you have each other, you'll be just fine. So, lean on each other, be kind, and celebrate my life when I'm gone." We all nod somberly.

"And somebody better kiss that handsome Joel since I'll never get the chance," she jokes, and we all manage to laugh through our tears.

We continue to cuddle with Mama until she drifts off again, and it feels like exactly what all of us needed, even Regina—especially Regina. After she's fallen asleep, we gather the plates and head to the kitchen to clean up.

We clean in silence, all of us overcome by the realization that Mama will be permanently gone from our lives pretty soon here. Once everything is cleaned, we all take a seat at the dining room table.

"Mama's right," I say.

"About someone needing to kiss Joel?" Trulia asks.

"No," I roll my eyes. "About the three of us being all we have. We can't keep fighting like this. We need each other, and we're going to need each other like never before after Mama passes."

"I agree," Regina says, smiling at me. I smile back. "I'm sorry," she admits.

"I'm sorry too…"

"Aww, okay now hug it out!" Trulia shouts. Reggie and I groan and roll our eyes at her.

"I really am going to miss her…" I say, tears forming again.

"At least we have all of our memories of her… those will never die," says Trulia.

"Yeah… nothing is going to be the same though, ever. You guys, I see Mama almost every single day. She's the one I call when something happens at the bakery and I don't know what to do. She's the one I call when I can't seem to get a recipe right, or when someone puts in an absurd cake order at The Muffin Top. She's the one I've spent every single holiday and birthday with my entire life… what am I going to do without her?" I sob.

"You'll call us instead; you'll spend the rest of the holidays and birthdays with us. That's what we're here for, duh," Regina says, coming over to me and pulling me into an embrace. Trulia joins us.

"I love you guys," Tru says.

"I love you guys too," we both respond.

We hug for a long time, and it feels good. It's the first time in a long time that the three of us have had a talk like this, or even said I love you to one another.

"Reggie do you want to come back to my place with Tru and I tonight? We can all have a sleepover together. It'll be just like the old days."

"You know what? Fuck it. Yes, I would love to do that."

"Yay!"

The three of us pile into my car and stop at Reg's hotel, so that she can grab her clothes and toiletries. Once we're back at my place, we grab all the pillows and blankets we can find, before all three of us pile into my bed.

Despite the overwhelmingly raw grief I feel, I'm able to put that aside for a few hours and just have a good night with my sisters. I fall asleep hoping that we have many more nights like this together in our future.

joel

Today I'm stopping by the bakery. It'll be my first time seeing her since—well, since my face was in between her legs. It'll be interesting to see how the two of us interact after seeing each other naked.

As I'm getting dressed for the day, I find myself caring a little more about my appearance—not that I didn't care before, but for some reason I feel the need to really try to look good today. Maybe I just don't want Bridgid to look at me and regret what we did.

I head into the office to take care of my responsibilities there before heading to the bakery. Once I'm done, I hop in my car and drive to the Muffin Top. I'm feeling a little extra giddy.

When I arrive, I feel the butterflies in my stomach before I even get out of the car. Trying to ignore them, I enter the bakery.

"Joel! It's good to see you again," Trulia greets me.

"Hello, good to see you do. Hope everyone's doing well."

Regina pulls me aside right away.

"Hey, I just want to apologize for what happened the last time we all sat down together. That was completely my fault, and you did nothin' wrong. I'm sorry."

"Listen, it's not a problem at all. This is my job. I witness people breaking down and getting into fights all the time —it's just part of the grieving process. I hope you know that you have absolutely nothing to be sorry for."

Regina gives me a hug, and we rejoin the rest of the sisters.

"Joel! Let's get you something to eat! I know you didn't actually get to have anything last time you were here, I'm sorry about that," Bridgid says.

"Oh, it's okay—I ate afterwards," I tell her, making eye contact for the first time. She slightly bites her bottom lip, suppressing a smile. I wonder if she got what I meant.

"So, Joel, Mama called you handsome last night!" Trulia informs me.

My face turns bright red.

"Tru! Oh my god, you weren't supposed to tell him that!" Bridgid says, faking a punch to Trulia's arm.

"*What?* It's fine, the woman's seventy-two. Besides, I'm sure he gets it all the time."

Bridgid rolls her eyes, and I laugh. It's funny seeing her squirm like this.

The girls bring me a cup of fresh coffee, exactly the way it was made last time, and they set down a big platter of pastries in the middle of our table. I immediately grab one and devour it, knowing it will make Bridgid happy to see.

Once we've all eaten a little something, we begin discussing the arrangement options again. The girls seem to have all calmed down a *lot*, but Regina still seems to want things her way.

"I just don't understand why we have to give Mama the cheapest options. She deserves better than that."

"Yes, but this is exactly what she asked for. Don't you want to honor her wishes?" Trulia asks.

"Of course, I do, but I also want to honor her *memory*, and these options just don't seem to be doing that."

"Honestly, guys?" Bridgid jumps in. "There's nothing in this world that can actually honor the memory of Mama.

No arrangement in the universe could do that. We will honor her in different ways, by remembering her and talking about her, and carrying on her legacy."

The girls nod, and we're all silent for a moment while Regina looks through more options. I'm honestly surprised at how wise Bridgid is every time she opens her mouth. It truly amazes me. The butterflies return.

I grab another pastry, hoping that will help with these flips my stomach is doing. But I know very well that having a full stomach won't take this feeling away.

Although Bridgid and I have both remained completely professional throughout this meeting, I still catch her sneaking glances at me out of the corner of my eye—and I'm sure she can see me doing the same. It isn't awkward, but you could cut the lingering tension with a knife.

Regina continues to shoot down all of the affordable options, she keeps going for the more expensive stuff. I see this happen a lot when it comes time to make these decisions. It often doesn't end well.

Suddenly Bridgid's phone rings.

"Oh, I should take this," she says, answering her phone and walking into her office in a hurry.

I watch her go, remembering everything that happened in that office when I was last here.

'*Focus, Joel,*' I tell myself.

The three of us sit in silence while Bridgid is gone. I sip my coffee. After a little while, I start to get worried. I look over and see her in deep conversation, pacing around her office. This doesn't look like it's a good phone call…

bridgid

My phone rings, and it's Mama's nurse Raul. Not wanting to worry my sisters in case it's nothing, I take the phone call into my office without telling them who it is.

"Raul? Is everything okay?"

"No… Bridgid you should prepare yourself; your mother is really struggling right now."

"Oh no…what's happening?"

"I think she's about to have another heart attack. She woke up today even worse than I've seen her in weeks."

"Wait—if she's been like this since this morning—then why are you just now calling me now?"

"I'm sorry, I didn't want to get you guys all scared and worried if it turned out to just be a bad morning. But this is more than just a bad

morning, Bridgid. I think it's time… you guys should get here… now."

"Okay… I'm sorry Raul, thank you. Should we bring anything? Or call anyone? Is there anything we can do?"

"No, just get here as soon as possible. The rest we will worry about later. Right now, you three just need to be here with her."

"Okay… okay, we're on our way." I hang up.

This cannot be happening. I don't believe it. It can't possibly be time yet. There's just no way. My sisters only just got here; they haven't had enough time with her…. I haven't gotten enough time with her. There's so much more I want to say to her, so much more I want to do with her. I need to tell her how much I appreciate her and everything she's done for me. I need to show her how much I love her.

I wipe any runway tears off of my face, and compose myself, not wanting to freak anyone out, before heading back to our table to give them the news. Joel is the first one I make eye contact with when I walk out. He looks worried, and when we lock eyes, I can tell that he knows what I'm about to say. I wish I didn't have to tell them this. Why does it always have to be me?

"Bee is everything okay? What was that about?" Regina asks.

"Guys… that was Raul. He says that Mama woke up in really bad shape this morning, and that she's deteriorating. He thinks it's because she's about to have another heart attack—and if that happens, she won't come back this time. So, he said we need to get there, now…"

"Oh my god…is he sure? Is that all he said?"

"Yes… it's time…" I begin to sob, even though no tears are coming out. Joel jumps up.

"Why don't you guys head there, and we'll lock up and be right behind you," he offers. Thank god for Joel. He always knows exactly what to do. My sisters nod, grab their things, and rush out without another word.

As soon as they're gone, my knees give out and I fall to the floor. Joel drops his papers and rushes to me, but I'm sobbing so hard that I barely notice him next to me. He pulls me to his chest, holding me close while I shake, tears rushing out at a speed I didn't even know was possible.

"What am I going to do without her Joel, what am I going to do? How am I going to wake up every day knowing I can't call her? How am I going to run this place without her?" I gesture to the kitchen.

He starts rocking me back and forth, combing his fingers through my hair, remaining silent. I look up at him.

"I can't do this, Joel… I can't. I can't do this…please make this stop."

"You can… you *can* do this. You have me, you have your sisters, and we'll be here every step of the way."

"I don't need *you* or my sisters; I need my *mother!*"

"Hey, hey it's okay… it's going to be okay. Just let it out…"

"It's not going to be okay… she's my *mother*, I *need* her. There's so much more I have to say to her, Joel…"

"I know… but trust me, anything you think you have to tell her—she already knows. And just because she is going to leave this earth… doesn't mean she won't still be with you every single day."

"You think she'll still be with me?"

"Absolutely, every single day. Just like I know that my mom is with *me* every day."

"I hope so… I really hope you're right Joel…"

I grab hold of his shirt, pulling him closer to me, and cry until I'm gasping for air. After a little while, I begin to calm down, realizing that I'm wasting time, and that I need to get to Mama fast if I want to say goodbye. I jump up, and rush to the kitchen.

"Bridgid, where are you going?" Joel shouts after me.

"I need to close up; I need to get to Mama. We're wasting time!"

"Okay, okay tell me what to do. I'll help."

I tell him what to do, and we rush around trying to get this done as fast as we can. Not that any of this really matters—I could honestly just leave everything—but I'm procrastinating what I have to go and do…

The two of us continue closing up, he grabs all of his paper that are scattered all across the floor, and stuffs them in his folder. We lock up, and head outside.

joel

BRIDGID AND I RUSH AROUND TRYING TO CLOSE UP AS fast as we can. I've never seen her like this, and it really scares me. I don't feel right parting ways with her right now. After we lock up, I decide to offer her a ride to Mama's house—my stomach turns at the thought of her driving herself anywhere in her current state.

"Hey uh, look—I wouldn't feel right letting you drive yourself right now—I think it's best if I take you."

"Actually yeah, can you? I can barely think right now—I don't want my sisters to have to go to two funerals in one week," she says.

"Sure, hop in," I motion to the passenger side of my car.

She goes back to double check that the bakery doors are indeed locked, before getting into my car.

"Thank you," she says once we're on our way.

"No problem."

The rest of the drive is completely silent, save for a few sniffles coming from Bridgid. Other than that, she doesn't say a word—and I don't push her to. I know exactly what she's going through right now, because it was my grief counselor that drove me when I had to say goodbye to my own mother.

I just wish that there was more that I could do to help her. I remind myself that I know from experience that the only thing I can really do is just be here.

As soon as we arrive, Bridgid jumps out of the car and runs in. I hesitate to follow her—I'm not really sure if this is my territory. I'm not really sure if I'm invited. After mulling it over, I decide to wait a little bit and let them have their family moment, and then afterwards I'll go in and just be there for grief support if they need it.

In the meantime, I take a seat in the red chair next to the front door. My feelings for Bridgid aside, this case has really gotten to me. Maybe that's because it's so similar to what happened to me, many years ago.

My mother died about five years ago now. She had metastatic skin cancer, and they found it six months before she died. It had been growing for years, so by the time they found it and diagnosed it—she had no chance. All we could do was wait. They tried some experimental treatment, but it didn't work, and so she was moved to hospice where I would visit her. It was terrible seeing her in that place for her last few months. It was incredibly hard to watch.

After she died, I really didn't think I could go on. She was the only person I had, the only person I loved so deeply. I was numb for months on end, but my grief counselor, Nathan, worked so hard to pull me out of that darkness. I'm so grateful to him, and I'll do the same thing for Bridgid—and her sisters—if need be. I'll do everything I can.

Of course, I still miss my mother every single day. I think about her all the time, and I even still cry about it sometimes. But I no longer feel numb. I no longer feel as if there's nothing left for me in this world, and that I can't go on. I know that my mother is looking down on me, watching me live my life. And I know that she's proud.

My mother was always so supportive of me. Even when I messed up—she was right there to help pick me back up again and help me come back even stronger. Everyone deserves someone like that in their lives. Someone who's there no matter what, and never gives up on them, no matter how hard things get. I find myself wanting to be that person for Bridgid.

Finally, I decide it's time to head inside—just in case they need me. When I walk in, it feels different. The energy in the house has changed. I walk down the hall to Mama's room and join them inside. I stand quietly in the back of the room with Raul while they all say their goodbye's. I'm usually not here for this part with my clients, and it's one of the saddest moments I've ever witnessed in my life. Even Raul and I start to cry as Mama's last breaths near.

bridgid

"She's still awake, but she is very weak and struggling to breathe," Raul says to me as I rush into the house. "I think she has been waiting for you, before she passes."

I nod to him and go down the hall to Mama's room. On either side of the bed sit my two sisters. They each have one of Mama's hands and they are whispering something to her that I can't hear. Tru looks up at me and gives me a sad shake of her head.

"Mama, look who is here. It's Bridgid," Reggie says. Mama opens her eyes, just enough to see me, and a faint smile crosses her lips. Tru gets up and walks to the window, making room for me to take her place. I tentatively sit on the end of the bed not wanting to jolt her, but hoping to connect with her just one more time.

"Oh mama, we love you so, so much. Isn't it great that all of your daughters are here to tell you how much we love you," I say, as I try to hold back the tears. She tries to look at all of us as her breath gets shallower. But it is too much for her and she closes her eyes again.

Knowing how much her faith means to her, I begin to say a simple prayer, hoping that she can still hear me. Ironically, it also calms me down a little. Even though I have given up religion myself, years ago, I take some comfort in the words that are so familiar.

I happen to look up and catch Reggie rolling her eyes at Tru. *'I know, big sister, you think I'm a hypocrite, but I don't care. This is for Mama, and I want to believe she can hear me,'* I think to myself as I continue the prayer. I place my hand on Mama's forehead and brush back her hair. This is too much for me, and I finish the prayer and get up to walk away.

That's when I happen to see Joel…..good, sweet Joel. He is standing in the corner of Mama's room, next to Raul. Our eyes meet and he gives me such an empathetic look that I want to go to him and just melt in his arms. But, I simply smile at him in thanks and turn my attention back to Mama.

Reggie, at this point, has lost all of her cold superiority, and has placed her head on Mama's chest and is quietly sobbing. Tru and I just look at each other in disbelief and wait for what seems like the inevitable.

Finally, after what seems like an eternity, Reggie lifts her head.

"I think she has passed. I can't hear her heart anymore," she informs us.

We all freeze and look at each other not knowing what to do next. I decide to speak up.

"Joel is here. Perhaps he can do whatever he's supposed to do to make it official."

Joel joins us at Mama's bed and makes the final determination that Mama is no longer on this earth with us anymore. I just stare at her in shock, as my sisters and I stand around the bed, bewildered.

"Why don't each of you have a little alone time with your mother. This way you can have your own private time to grieve with her," Joel says, looking at each of us for approval.

"Reggie, you're the oldest. Why don't you stay, and we will all meet up in the parlor and wait for you there," I say. "Trulia and I will take our turn after you. Take as much time as you need." I lead Tru and Joel down the hallway to the parlor.

When we get there, Raul is still there and looks at me with questioning eyes. I tell him that Mama has passed, and we share a little hug. Then, I tell him that he should go home and that I will take care of things from here.

"Well, I think I need a little drink," Tru says. "Does Mama still keep any alcohol in the house for special occasions?"

"I'll get it," I say. "I know where she hides everything in this house."

When I come back Joel and Tru are sitting on the couch. He is holding her hand and speaking to her in such soothing tones. She is nodding her head and trying to keep up a brave facade. I watch them for a while with affection until they both notice me.

"I found some old peach schnapps" I say, as I hold up the bottle and some glasses. "Will that do?" Trulia looks up and laughs.

"Anything will do, at this point", she says.

We pour the drinks just as Reggie comes back into the room. We pour one for her too and we all do a little toast to the amazing woman who is no longer with us.

"I'm going to get some air on the porch," Reggie says, as Trulia heads down to the bedroom to pay her last respects.

"Thank you for being here," I say to Joel, as I take his hand. "You are a sweet man." He smiles at me and we sit in silence waiting for my turn with Mama.

Finally, Tru comes out and I make my way back to the bedroom. I stand next to her bed for a moment before I bend over and give her a soft kiss on her forehead. She looks so at peace, and it comforts me.

"Oh Mama, I am going to miss you so much. Thank you for making me your favorite. I always knew I was. And I love you for it."

When I get back to the parlor my sisters and I all have a group hug, and it feels so right to share this grief with them. After a few moments we all hold hands and suddenly remember that Joel is still with us.

"Shall I call Hibberts and have them send the hearse?' I hear Joel say. I look at him and nod. There is nothing else to say.

joel

IT'S THE DAY AFTER MAMA PASSED AWAY, AND THE SISTERS and I are supposed to meet at the funeral home to finally sit down and make the choices that need to be made once and for all.

Last night was horrible for everyone involved, but I'm glad that I was there to provide some support when they needed it. Seeing Bridgid like that was hard—it was like a small piece of her died along with her mother. It's especially hard to watch considering I know exactly what they're all going through right now.

I hope today goes well and everyone is able to decide on something without arguing, because ultimately there really isn't any time left for that. It's going to be hard, but once this whole process is over, we can celebrate the life of a wonderful woman, and the girls can start properly grieving and moving on with their lives.

An hour before we're supposed to meet, I head to the funeral home to get ready. I pulled some more expensive options for Regina since she seems to want to go that route, while also keeping some more humble options in the mix as well. Once I'm all prepared for my meeting with them, I make a cup of coffee and take a seat on the couch in my office until they arrive.

I try not to think about Bridgid in any way other than as a client, because despite what happened in her office a few days ago… that really is all she is, my client. And I need to be respectful of that and treat her that way from now on. I'm honestly pretty disappointed in myself for slipping up so much with her, it's really not like me to be in a situation like this.

Whatever I feel for Bridgid—while it is very real for me, it is incredibly inappropriate. I need to remind myself of that and channel the professional man that I usually am. I contemplate this until the sisters pull up, and I bring them into my office with all of the options spread out on the table for them.

"How are you girls doing?" I ask. It may seem like a stupid question because of course, their mother just died —they're doing horrible. But it's important to ask these questions and get them talking about what they're feeling.

"I'm doing okay, I woke up today feeling pretty numb. Last night was really hard, but I think I've come to terms with the fact that it was her time, and that she was okay with that—so maybe I should be too," Trulia says.

"Although I think it will take me a while to get to that place… I totally agree with you…" Bridgid admits, wiping a stray tear from her cheek.

We all look to Regina.

"Honestly? I think I'm still in a bit of denial. Even though I saw it with my own eyes—it's just hard for me to process and admit to myself that she really is gone… I think I'll take your advice and seek out some help soon."

"Good, I'm really glad you told us that. All of you. It really is very important to express these emotions out loud. Even if you feel the same thing every day, expressing them can help take away the power those emotions have over you. I hope that the three of you continue to do that with each other. Oftentimes when family members lose one of their own, it can be easy to separate after such a loss. But I think it would really benefit you three specifically to stay together and lean on one another." They all nod.

"Okay, now onto the reason we're here today. I pulled a few more options in addition to the ones you have already looked at, since nothing really seemed to be catching your eyes."

"Well, *I'm* perfectly fine with choosing the options that Mama asked for," Bridgid says, glancing at Regina tentatively. Regina sighs, taking a deep breath before opening her mouth.

"Okay, I've thought about this a lot over the past few days, and especially this morning. And I think I need to explain to you guys why exactly I want Mama to have more than these basic options. So just hear me out, okay?" Once Bridgid and Trulia give her the okay, she continues.

"Look, the reason I keep asking for these more expensive options is because I think that Mama only picked the economy options because she didn't want to be a burden on any of us. You guys know how humble Mama was, and she never would have asked for something nicer, knowing that it would cost us more money—that's just who she is—was. But I want to celebrate Mama's life with nicer funerary choices than she ever would have asked for. Just because she picked *these* options, doesn't mean that she actually liked and wanted that. And I know I've been a bitch about it—believe me, I know. I really wasn't trying to be—it just frustrated me that no one was taking what Mama might have actually wanted into consideration."

Bridgid and Trulia are silent for a moment, looking at each other and back to Regina.

"Reggie, I understand that you just want to show how much you and all of us loved Mama. I know you just want to show your appreciation for her through this...

but Mama's not here anymore. She wouldn't have cared about how nice her funeral was, all she would care about is that we all got along and celebrated her. And besides… Reg, we really can't afford anything more than this, and you just lost your job, so I know you can't either," Trulia breaks it to her.

Regina seems to think for a moment before responding.

"You're right, I did just lose my job. But I'm already looking for my next position, and not only that—but I happen to have a very large savings that I can use for this. Just let me do this…"

"Okay," Bridgid speaks up. "You pick out what you think embodies Mama the best—nothing *too* expensive though. We'll look at it, and if you pay the difference then we can do it that way. I can see how much this clearly means to you."

Everyone agrees, and Regina shows them what she has in mind. It ends up being a lot more expensive than their original budget, but Regina agrees to pay the whole difference. It's nice to see them all finally agreeing on something with no arguing or anything.

Chapter Twenty-Three

bridgid

WE ALL FINALLY AGREE TO GIVE REGGIE WHAT SHE WANTS and give Mama a more expensive funeral. I really believe that Mama truly just wanted these options, but I realized that for Regina it isn't about that. This is just her way of coping, and if this is what she needs to make herself feel better—let her have it. We can all take any help we can get right now to feel better.

After everything is finalized, we discuss what to do next. Someone has to go with Joel to pick out Mama's final outfit.

"Honestly, guys? I just want to go back to my hotel," Regina states.

"I'll go with you. I don't really want to be alone right now," Trulia admits. But I know Trulia, and so I know that what she really meant was that she doesn't want *Reggie* to be alone right now.

We're both a little worried about her—especially after she fully admitted that she's in denial about Mama. And when the denial phase passes—she definitely shouldn't be alone for that.

"Okay, that's fine with me. I'll go with Joel then." It's probably for the best that I pick out Mama's outfit anyways, considering I was the closest to her.

Regina and Trulia take off, and it's just me and Joel.

"This is going to be extremely hard," I confide in him.

"It will be… but you're strong enough, and I'll be right there the whole time." I nod.

"Do you want to stop at the bakery for some coffee before we go?"

"Umm, *absolutely*—I would *never* turn down your coffee."

This causes me to giggle. I think it's cute how excited he gets over my coffee, and that he had only ever had straight black coffee before. We get into his car and stop in the Muffin Top. It's not that I really wanted coffee *that* bad—I'm just procrastinating what we have to go do. Even though I'm starting to come to peace with Mama being gone, I know that it will still take me a lot of adjusting and it's still very hard. I just want all of this to be over with already.

The two of us take a seat on a small bench outside of the bakery and sip our coffee. I sip mine extra slow, he of course gulps his down in minutes.

"You're supposed to *enjoy* it, you pig!"

"I *was* enjoying it—why do you think I drank it so damn quickly?"

"Ugh, fair enough," I give in.

After a few more minutes, we get back in the car and head to Mama's.

"It's so beautiful here," Joel points out.

"Really? I guess I don't really notice, I've been here my entire life."

"Ugh, lucky."

"You must really hate California, if you think this small town is that amazing."

"It's not that I hate it—Cali is stunningly beautiful. But like you, I lived there my whole life—I enjoy this change of scenery."

"You're crazy. I would die to have grown up in California."

"Eh, it's not all it's cracked up to be."

"Well, I don't believe you. I'll have to go see it and decide for myself one day."

We make small talk for the rest of the drive. The more I talk, the less time I have to think about Mama. Joel seems to drive slower, as if he can sense that I've been procrastinating.

Finally, we arrive. Neither of us moves. We sit in silence for a few minutes, Joel staring out the window, me staring at my shoes. I can't make my legs move to get out of the car. I can't make my eyes move to look up at the house.

"I can't do it… I'm not ready…"

"Okay…"

"Can you take me somewhere else? I don't even care where—just anywhere but here."

"I know a place," he says, and we pull off.

I don't know why, but I just couldn't do it. Not yet. Going into that house, knowing it was the last place any of us saw Mama alive… I just can't. After the horror of watching her die in there last night… how am I supposed to walk in those doors, walk in her room, and pick out something for her to wear to her funeral? How is anyone expected to do these types of things?

joel

I KNOW EXACTLY WHERE TO TAKE HER. I HOP ONTO I-35, and we drive for a little over twenty minutes before pulling into the city of Salado. I drive us to Salado Creek, a place that I come and visit from time to time when I just need a moment to myself. I'm glad I get to share this place with someone finally—but especially with Bridgid.

"You know, it really blows my mind that I know of more cool spots around here than you do, when you're the one who's lived here your entire life."

"I guess Mama and I were just never the traveling type. She always stayed in one place, and wherever she went—I went. Wow… it's so weird to be using past tense when talking about her now…"

"Yeah, that takes a while to get used to. But after a while it will become more normal and you almost won't even notice you're doing it."

"Thanks. I'm glad I have you, someone who's been through this before and can help me navigate these new waters."

"Me too. And speaking of waters—get out, you're going to love this," I say once we've parked.

Salado Creek is one of the most beautiful places I've witnessed since moving here. The water is beautiful and clean, and there's a lovely bridge you can walk across—it's a very historical-feeling place.

"How did you find this place? It looks wonderful!" Bridgid asks.

"I've always been an explorer! Everywhere I go I look for places like this that bring me peace. Having a job like mine, you need things that bring you peace to help separate the grief I feel at work from my real life."

"That makes sense, you're a really smart guy you know," Bridgid states.

"Thank you, I get that from my mom," I tell her. She nods.

We walk along the creek quietly for a few minutes before she breaks the silence.

"Tell me about your mother."

We take a seat on the huge limestone rocks next to the Creek with our feet dangling in the water before I begin.

"Mother was perfect. Her favorite thing to do was paint—everywhere we traveled, she brought her easel and painted whatever was in front of us. And she was really good at it too. I always wished she had pursued it as a career—but she always said she never wanted it to become work because she loved it so much. She didn't want that love to go away."

"Where did you guys travel to?"

"Oh everywhere—by the time I was eighteen, we had traveled to at *least* fifteen different states. We went to canyons, national forests, waterfalls, beautiful trails, amazing beaches, and even hiked up a couple of mountains together."

"Wow… how did you guys afford that? That sounds expensive!"

"You know—it really wasn't. Mom was a part time flight attendant, and so she got a lot of free flights from the airline she worked for. So, we would fly to different parts of the country, visit the places we wanted to go, stay in cheap motels, and fly back the next day. It was really amazing, and we were really lucky to be able to do that. Especially together. Those are memories I'll never ever forget."

"Your mother sounds amazing. She sounds like a very adventurous and free-spirited woman."

"She was. Every single person who met her fell in love. She was so bright and happy all the time. That's what made it even harder when she got sick—it was really hard to see such a charismatic person become so ill and not be able to do any of the things she loved. She didn't deserve that. I try to tell myself that mom lived her life to the absolute fullest, and she didn't miss out on anything. I know she wouldn't want me to let her death ruin my life. She would want me to continue doing exactly what makes me happy. She would want me to remember her in a positive way, and not let the memory of her bring me sadness."

"That's a really positive way to look at it. I hope I can get to that place someday."

"You will. Trust me, it just takes time. But you know in your heart that Mama would not want you to let this change you forever. She will be looking down on you, and she wants to see you live a happy and full life."

"You're right. I don't want Mama to see me go into a depression. I have to try and stay positive for her."

"Exactly. We owe it to them for the amazing lives they gave us." She nods.

"What about your dad? Did he go everywhere with you guys?"

"No, actually I haven't seen my father since I was about five years old. He left around the time when my mother got her job as a flight attendant. My mom never really talked much about him. She didn't exactly speak ill of him, but I could tell her that he really hurt her, so I never pushed her on the subject."

"Do you want to know more about him now that your mom has passed?"

"Honestly? I've never been interested in knowing him —*especially* after my mom passed. The fact that he could leave such an amazing woman to raise her child all alone is something I don't think I could ever forgive him for."

"I understand."

We sit for a little while longer, Watching the sun go down. It's a beautiful day and there are so many colors in the sky, my mother would have loved to paint this scene.

"We should probably get going now, don't you think?" Bridgid asks.

"Actually, do you mind waiting a little bit? There's something I want to show you."

Bridgid looks a bit uneasy.

"I don't know… it's getting pretty dark out here."

"I can use the flashlight on my phone to find our way back to the car when it gets darker. Plus, I've been here like a million times—I know exactly where everything is."

"Okay, okay—we can stay a little longer. But this thing you have to show me better be good."

"Oh, trust me, it's magical."

Chapter Twenty-Five

bridgid

I REALLY ENJOY SPENDING THIS TIME WITH JOEL. I LOVE learning new things about him and watching him talk about things that he's so passionate about. Sitting here with him all alone at this beautiful place really makes me think about what a life with him would be like. I'm not saying I necessarily *want* to have a life with him—but it's kind of hard to not think about it when we spend moments together like this.

I love hearing him talk about his mom and what she was like. They were obviously very close like Mama and I. Thinking about him going through what I am right now makes me incredibly sad. He's so put together all the time that it's hard to imagine him ever being in a bad place.

Having Joel around during this horrible time in my life really makes me feel less alone. He knows exactly how to make me feel understood. I think the fact that he has been through this exact same thing makes me feel a lot more comfortable around him than I feel with anyone else right now. Overall, I'm just really thankful to have someone like him around.

It really helps to see someone who has been through this doing so good in their life. Seeing how Joe handles himself without his mother, while knowing how much he misses her, makes me feel like I can actually get through this. It's almost inspiring. I will forever be grateful to him for that.

This place really is beautiful, and I think that if I spend more time around Joel, I will visit many more places just as beautiful. He's definitely right—being out in nature like this is very therapeutic. It might sound silly, but it really does bring me peace. I think Mama would have loved it here.

We sit by the creek for a little while longer, while he tells me more about his mother. He tells me about how the only thing she knew how to cook was spaghetti, and so that's what they ate most nights if they didn't order out. All of his stories about her are so hilarious that it makes me sad that I can't meet her. I think I would have loved her.

A half hour has gone by and I'm not really sure what it is that he needs to show me so badly—but apparently it requires it to be dark outside. To be honest, I'm a little scared.

Finally, the sun has completely set and the only light around us is from the moon. I look over at him waiting for something to happen when all of a sudden thousands of fireflies emerge, seemingly out of nowhere to light up the night. Joel grabs my hand, pulling me up and walking us towards them.

I look around in awe, and it feels like I'm in an actual fairy tale. The beauty of it all soothes my soul.

"Oh my god… Joel this really is so amazing and was definitely worth the wait…"

I look around us, mesmerized by all the little lights flying around us. it baffles me that a place like this exists and I never knew about it.

"I want to come here every single night," I laugh.

"That can be arranged," he jokes.

"Let's dance!" I shout.

He grabs my hands, and we traipse around under the trees together. Even though there's no music—dancing has never felt so good. Finally, we get tired and topple into the grass together.

"Thank you for this… seriously. Thank you, Joel."

"Anytime Madam. Are you feeling hungry?"

"Actually, I kind of am, but I don't really feel up to going out anywhere."

"Everything is much easier after a good meal," he says. "What are you in the mood for?"

"You know I could really go for some barbeque right now…"

"Perfect, I actually know a barbecue place that will blow your mind."

"Of course, you do, you seem to know a place for just about anything," I laugh.

"That's because I do… so I'll call in an order, and we can eat it at your apartment?" he asks.

"Oh, actually I don't think I'm quite ready to return to that reality yet."

"Okay that's totally fine," he shrugs. "We can take it back to my place then."

"Oh, that would be perfect thank you."

"No problem, let's head back to the car and place this order—I'm fucking starving."

Joel calls in an order and we take off. During the car ride there we turn on some music, and he gives me a little concert. It's so adorable seeing him let loose like this that I can't help but join in. Hanging out with him like this is actually turning out to be quite fun.

When we arrive at the barbecue place, Joel runs in and grabs the food, putting it in the backseat of his car before heading to his place. For a second, I wonder if it's weird that I'm about to go to Joel's house. After some thought, I decide that it's not. Besides, we both know where we stand after what happened with us in my office—so it's not like it's even like that. At least that's what I tell myself…

joel

Bridgid and I have a blast singing together on the way to my house. It helps take away the nerves I have at the thought of Bridgid being in my home. When we finally arrive, I'm so hungry that it takes everything in me to not dig in before we even get inside. I probably ordered enough barbecue for about six people—I didn't know what she liked, so I ended up getting a little bit of everything just in case.

As soon as we enter, my cat Griselda jumps from her tower and lands at my feet, meowing furiously. I'm usually never home this late, so I'm sure she's quite mad.

"Oh Grissy, don't worry—I'm here to feed you," I tell her.

I set down our takeout on the coffee table in the living room, before heading straight to Grissy's bowl and filling it up. She turns and yells at me one more time before digging in. Bridgid is laughing the whole time, finding humor out of the fact that my cat actually scolds me.

"This is standard behavior for cats—we don't own them, they own us."

"Riiight, you just don't want to admit that you're whipped," she jokes.

"How could I not be—Griselda is a queen. Are you telling me that you don't like cats?"

"Eh, they're okay—I just find it cute that you have one."

For some reason this makes me blush, hearing her call me cute makes my heart flutter a little. I turn away and start getting out all of the takeout boxes, displaying all of the food.

"What the fuck—how much did you order?" She questions.

"Ha-ha—um, a lot… I wasn't sure what you would like."

"Oh, I'll eat pretty much everything—I'm only picky when it comes to sweets. I mean, I kind of have to be the owner of a bakery."

"Well, I guess I'll have leftovers for about two weeks then," I laugh.

Before diving in, I give Bridgid a quick tour of my home. She inspects each room and seems to approve.

"I really like this place, it's perfect for you," she says after the tour is over.

"What's that supposed to mean?" I ask, wondering if I should be offended.

"No no, nothing bad. I just mean that it's exactly what I would have pictured your home to be like. I love that you have all of your travel photos with your mother displayed in each room. I'm not sure if I could have photos of Mama everywhere reminding me of what happened to her."

"Yeah, I can see why you would say that… I felt like that at first but honestly it makes me happy to see them every day. Eventually you will get to a place where seeing her or thinking about her doesn't hurt. The only thing that will hurt is the fact that she's gone."

"You're so strong, Joel," she says, a small but warm smile on her face.

"Thank you… you are too you know—whether you see it yet or not."

We head back into the living room to dig into our barbecue. We fill up our plates and sit on the couch together. A couple bites in, she gasps.

"Oh my god Joel… I think this is the best food I've had in a really long time. What was the place called again? And why have you kept this a secret?"

I laugh at how amazed she is.

"It's called Billy Bob's BBQ. They're actually known for having the best ribs in the county."

"Wow… I feel like I'm not even a real Texan…"

"I completely agree with that statement, I've only been here for a little while and I'm already more of a Texan than you."

"Oh shut up, you're an "explorer"—this shit is right up your alley."

We laugh for a moment, and Griselda hops up on the couch and curls up in my lap. I can practically feel Bridgid swooning over seeing us cuddling. I look over to see her watching us peacefully, a look on her face that I can't quite name.

She slowly reaches up and caresses my face, a serious expression taking over her smile. I stiffen at her touch, remembering how we agreed that nothing would happen between us again. I would never want to disrespect her, but if she's initiating it…

She pulls me closer, pushing her lips against mine. The minute we touch, I allow myself to admit how much I missed how this feels. How could I not? I pull her into my lap, wanting, no *needing* her to be as close as possible.

As soon as she's in my lap, it's like we pick off right where we left it. She grinds softly against me, letting her lips trail down my neck. I pull my shirt off, at the same time she pulls off hers. I can't wait any longer, I pick her up and carry her into my room, pushing her down onto the bed.

Chapter Twenty-Seven

bridgid

I'VE NEVER WANTED SOMEONE SO BADLY IN MY ENTIRE life. I've been thinking about what this would be like ever since the last time Joel and I had a moment together. He picks me up and takes me to his room, pushing me down onto the bed. I practically rip my bra off, revealing my perky breasts.

"You're so beautiful," Joel whispers.

"Let's pick up where we left off… I need you," I moan.

"Oh, you need me, huh?"

"Yes…"

He trails his fingers up my legs, pulling my leggings down when he reaches my waist.

"How badly do you need me?"

"Joel… enough teasing I can't take it," I whimper.

"Oh this? This is nothing…"

He runs his finger over my panties, right where my clit is hiding. Ever so gently rubbing his finger up and down my clit, he increases the torture. I fight the urge to moan, not wanting to show any signs of weakness.

He takes it one step further, bringing his face in between my legs, kissing, and licking up and down my inner thighs. He knows exactly what he's doing to me, and I love that… but I need to show him that I know exactly what I'm doing too.

I close my legs together, leaving him shocked. Pulling him down onto the bed with me, I rip off what's left of his clothes, revealing his rock hard cock. I kiss his neck, then his chest, all the way down until I get to his manhood. Then I stop, look at him, and without breaking eye contact I lick him, starting from the bottom up. He groans, and I know what he wants me to do. But I won't give it to him, not yet.

Sliding my hand along his shaft, I stroke him, while I bring my mouth down to his balls and suck on them. I bring him closer and closer to his climax with each stroke, but right when he's about to come, I stop.

"Bridgid…" he growls, covering his face with his hands.

Right then, I take his entire length into my mouth all at once, feeling his tip at the back of my throat. He gasps, and I grab his balls into one hand, massaging them as I slowly bob my head up and down.

Joel grabs a handful of my hair, pushing my head down faster. I give him what he wants and quicken my pace until I physically can't go any faster. I'm choking on him and I'm loving it—hearing his moans only gives me more incentive to keep going. A few moments later, he comes down my throat and lets out a loud groan, releasing my hair.

I chuckle at how out of breath he is, but I give him no time to recover. I rip off my panties, hop onto his cock, and immediately start bouncing at warp speed. All I can think about is everything this man has done for me and how much I want to please him. I've honestly never heard a man moan as loud as Joel does as I ride him— even in porn.

I put my hands on his chest and let my ass do the work, jiggling all around his cock. He grabs my ass and squeezes so hard I can't help but cry out. This only makes him smirk, and he slaps it even harder. God he's sexy. He violently thrusts upwards as I slide along is length, and we come together, before collapsing side by side.

"You're fucking amazing," he pants, running his fingers softly up and down my body.

"Tell me something I don't know."

"I want to fuck you again," he whispers into my ear, sending shivers down my spine.

Without waiting for my response, he turns me over onto my stomach. He puts one pillow under my stomach and pushes my legs together, leaving a very tight opening for him to enter me.

"Squeeze your legs together as tightly as you can," he grunts. I obey him.

I lie there on my stomach, squeezing my thighs together to create an even smaller opening. He pushes himself into my pussy inch by inch, moaning louder each time he gains new ground. Just when I think he's all the way in, he gives me even more. This position makes him feel even bigger than before, which is really saying something.

Finally, he pushes the rest of himself in all at once, causing me to cry out. He starts with quick, hard thrusts, pounding himself into me and pausing slightly after each one. Every thrust hits my g-spot perfectly, and after a few more I'm practically screaming. He grabs my hair and pulls my head back, bringing his mouth to my ear while he fucks me.

"You like that?"

I manage to choke out a response in between his thrusts, which seem to be gaining power. I squeeze my legs even tighter.

"Say it for me," he growls.

"I—like—it—" I sputter, eyes rolling to the back of my head

"Good girl."

His pace suddenly quickens, and he slams himself into me repeatedly, picking up more and more speed. I can't control myself, I grab onto the bed and let myself come, screaming louder than I even knew I could. He finishes inside of me, and I pull him down next to me and lay my head across his chest.

I'm completely speechless, all I can do is lie there in pure bliss. He draws circles on my back, completely clueless as to what he just did to me.

'*No sex will ever top this,*' I think to myself as I come back down to earth.

joel

I WAKE UP EARLY, LIKE I NORMALLY DO, AND ROLL OVER to gaze at this beautiful creature who is asleep in my bed. She looks so peaceful, and I am happy for her. After the rough week she has had she deserves a little down time. So, I decide to let her sleep for a while, and I head to the kitchen to make breakfast. I'm sure she will be hungry, since we didn't have time to finish that barbecue last night.

I get the coffee going and clean up the mess from last night. After I get an omelet started I hear her getting up and heading to the shower. Awhile later she appears in the doorway wearing one of my t-shirts and nothing else.

"Lordy, Lordy. You cook too?' she says, and she gives me a big hug. "You know, I'm still tingling from last night."

"Well, I hope you are hungry because I am making my special mushroom and spinach omelet."

"At this point I am just enjoying someone waiting on me for a change. I'd be happy with just a piece of toast," she says, as she plops down at the kitchen table.

After breakfast we stop by her apartment so that she can change her clothes before we head to her mother's house. I wait in the car for her and let my mind drift back to the night before.

'What was I thinking? Jumping into bed with a client? A client who is grieving?'

I try to put these thoughts out of my mind.

'I know it was wrong—but damn, it felt so good.'

When we get to her mom's house she hesitates before she opens the front door. I can tell she is steeling herself for whatever emotions are going to greet her. She realizes that it's the first time that her mom won't be a presence in the house. She looks back at me to get a little courage and gently enters.

When we get to her mom's bedroom she enters and then pauses at the bed, as if to feel if her spirit is still present. She turns around slowly and surveys the whole room, trying to take in every detail. Finally, she goes to her mom's vanity and sits. She picks up some of the jars of creme and opens them. She smiles as she picks up a hairbrush and pulls out a few strands of hair. I watch her from a distance, knowing she needs this time to process.

"Well, I guess we should get what we came here for," she finally says. "What type of dress should I pick out? Does it need to be black?"

"It should be something nice, but not too fancy," I tell her. "Make sure it is something that represents who she was. Maybe something simple, yet elegant."

"I wish we could bury her in her apron," she chuckles. "That's how I always think of her when I try to remember her now," she tells me, as she opens the closet door.

There are lots of dresses in the closet and she begins to look through them, one at a time. She takes her time and considers each one, trying to picture her mom laid out. Suddenly, she buries her face in one of the dresses and begins to sob.

"Oh Mama. Mama, I wish you were here to tell me what to do. You always knew what was best," she sobs, continuing to bury her face into the dress.

I come up behind her and gently put my arms around her waist and rest my head against hers. She turns in my embrace and continues to cry against my chest. Gradually, the tears subside, and she squeezes me tighter.

"I'm sorry," she says. " I was doing okay, and then Mama's smell got the best of me. And I lost it."

"You're doing fine," I tell her. "I would think you weren't normal if you went through your mom's things and didn't get emotional. Now, I don't have to worry about you being a freak."

She smiles and pushes me away, going back to the dresses and finally making a decision.

"I should get some of her jewelry too. She didn't have any on when she went," she says as she moves back to the vanity.

She opens up the jewelry box and tries on a few necklaces, until she finds one that is appropriate. Then she picks out a pair of shoes that would go with the dress.

"Wow, this is harder than I thought," she says as she puts everything into a small suitcase. "Maybe I should also grab Mama's box of papers while I'm here. I can go over them with my sisters when we are all at the bakery."

She goes to the bottom drawer of the dresser and pulls out a metal box. She obviously knew exactly where it was. She opens the box and stares at the contents.

"I wonder if Mama has a will in here," she whispers. "Mama said she was going to name me as executor, but I don't know if she ever got around to doing it. Maybe I should wait for my sisters before I go through any of this," she says before closing the box.

We drive to the bakery and Bridgid sits in the front seat without saying anything. She just stares at the box on her lap the whole way over. When we get there, I get out and open the door for her.

"I'll take the dress back to the funeral home and make sure that everything is taken care of. You don't have to worry about a thing," I say, as I help her out of the car.

"You are the kindest man I know," she says, before giving me a big kiss and walking away.

I watch her until she disappears into the bakery. Then I drive away, admitting to myself that I really do need this woman in my life more than I thought I ever would.

Chapter Twenty-Nine

bridgid

I GIVE JOEL A BIG HUG, AND HEAD INTO THE BAKERY TO meet with my sisters. I hope they didn't look out the window and see us together—I really don't feel like revealing my personal shit to them. My life is too complicated right now to have to explain it to my sisters. Hell, I don't even understand it myself, right now.

How do I explain how I got involved so fast with our Funeral Director's assistant? I'm sure that Tru would be okay with it, but I'm not sure about Reggie. She's been away so long, that honestly, I don't think I even know her anymore.

Luckily, they are sitting over in the corner drinking coffee. They seem to be involved in an intense conversation. They only look up when I approach the table and set down the box that I've been carrying.

"I brought Mama's box of important papers from the house. Give me a few minutes to check on the staff and see that things are okay, and then we can look things over," I say, heading to the kitchen to deal with any problems that may be brewing.

When I return fifteen minutes later, there are papers spread all over the table. And my sisters are looking rather grim.

"You better sit down. There are some things we need to discuss," Reggie says. "Did you know Mama had a will?"

"She talked about getting one done a few times, but I didn't know she went ahead and did it. You already looked at it?" They look at each other suspiciously, and then back to me.

"So, you didn't know she named you executor of the will?" Trulia asks, inquisitively.

"I had no idea," I state.

"Why would she name you as executor?" Reggie shouts. "I'm the oldest, and I'm the one who understands finance. What do you know about dealing with a probate?"

"Maybe it's because I'm the one who was there for her and took care of her when she was sick. Did you ever think of that?" I shout back, not wanting to be bullied by Reggie again.

"Why don't we all just chill out a second," says Tru. " If Mama was alive she would be ashamed to see us acting like this." Tru has always been the peacemaker in the family.

We all decide that we will go through everything in the box before we come to any family decisions. Mama's will was pretty simple. It left the Bakery business to me and the house and all of Mama's possessions to be divided equally between the three of us. The rest of the box was filled with a lot of bills that hadn't been paid yet.

"How come you get the business and a third of the house?" Reggie asks me.

"Because I've been here helping Mama run things while you were off doing your own thing. Besides, the business is just barely making it. We are three months behind on the rent. Mr. Feeny has been letting us slide because he likes Mama, and he knows that she has been sick. I'm not sure how much longer he will be that nice."

This shuts Reggie up for a while. She starts to add up the bills with a little calculator that she pulls out of her bag. She shakes her head and blows air through her teeth as she works her way through the pile of papers. Finally, she looks up, disgusted.

"Not only are there a shit load of bills here that have not been paid, but Mama took loans out against the house. She was mortgaged up to her eyeballs. You were around

Bridgid, how could you have let this get so bad?" She asks, looking straight at me.

"I didn't realize things were so bad! Mama always took care of the bills and kept all of that stuff pretty secret. Besides, I was too busy keeping the rest of the business running when Mama got sick."

"I have to call the bank and see how much is still left on these loans," Reggie says, and she get up from the table. She takes her cell phone with her and goes outside, leaving Tru and I to gather up the mess of papers that have been scattered.

"Just because her name is Regina, doesn't mean that she is the Queen," I say to Tru, when Reggie is out of earshot. "I mean, who does she think she is, coming back here and bossing everyone around?"

"That's just the way she always was, even when we were kids," Tru says. "I think it's just her insecurity. I imagine it's worse now that she got canned from her last job. Just let her have her say, and then do what you want. Don't forget, you are the executor."

I don't know if that last statement makes me feel better or worse. I don't have time to really think about it, because here comes Reggie with a head of steam. She looms over us with fire in her eyes.

"We are screwed. Screwed. Screwed. Screwed. How could she do this to us?" she says. Reggie was always a bit dramatic, but this time she seems scared.

"What happened?" Tru and I both say at once. I look over my shoulder to make sure that the staff is not overhearing this.

"Mama was taking out loans to fix up the house and to prop up the business. She has also been late in paying them off."

"What are you talking about?" I say. "It can't be that much, or she would have told me she was in trouble."

"You were always so naive, Bridgid," Reggie says, and she sits down, like the life has just gone out of her.

"Well, how much are we talking about?" Tru asks.

"With what's owed on the loans and all the outstanding bills, we're looking at...." Reggie pauses for effect.

"Around twenty thousand dollars..."

joel

AFTER DROPPING BRIDGID OFF AT THE BAKERY, I HEAD TO the funeral parlor to deliver Mama's dress and things. I find myself wishing I had stayed with Bridgid—she seemed very distracted and lost. But I want to get things started with her mom's funeral as fast as possible.

When I get to the parlor I take the dress to Helen. She is our most dependable employee, and I want to make sure there are no problems down the road.

"Helen, this is Mrs. Grant's dress and belongings. She and her family are very special clients, so I want you to make sure that she is given the attention she deserves. I am personally invested in how this funeral goes." She looks at me warily, and nods.

After I get the assurance that everything is in order, I head back out. I can't get Bridgid out of my head and I need to make sure that she is okay. So, I head back to the bakery to offer whatever support I can. These are very fragile times for a family, and maybe my experience can be beneficial.

When I enter the bakery, I see the three sisters are at a table in the corner having a very animated conversation. I weigh whether I should back out gracefully and give them some space. I see that Bridgid has noticed me out of the corner of her eye. We lock eyes for a moment, but she makes no indication for me to stay or leave. Just then, I hear Reggie's voice loud and clear.

"You are such a child, Bridgid," she says. "You are stuck in this small town, and you have no idea how the real-world works."

I figure now is the time to make myself known, and hopefully break the tension.

"Hi everyone," I say, innocently. " I hope I'm not interrupting anything. I just wanted to make sure that Bridgid didn't need me for anything else." Bridgid and Tru give me a friendly smile. But, Reggie looks like she wants to bite my head off.

" No, everything is good," Bridgid says. "We were just going over some little details about Mama's finances."

"Everything is good?" Reggie explodes. "Bridgid, if you got your head out of your ass you would know that everything is not good. Everything is *shit*."

"Well, listen. If you are having trouble paying the funeral expenses, maybe we can work out a payment plan over time that won't be too painful." I look at everyone expecting them to be grateful.

"That's very kind of you Joel," Trulia says. "But unfortunately, our problems go way beyond that."

"We wouldn't have these problems if Bridgid knew what the fuck she was doing," Regina screams. "Why didn't you keep on top of things, and not allow Mama to get so behind on her bills?"

Bridgid looks like she is about to cry.

"It's not my fault," Bridgid explains. "Mama was very secretive about her finances. I think she was too embarrassed to let me know what was going on. She didn't want me to think that she wasn't competent enough to run a business. She was a proud woman, you know that!"

"Well because of that, we are now the proud owners of a twenty-thousand-dollar debt!" Reggie spits out.

She gets up and heads to the restroom to blow off steam. The three of us look at each other, too stunned to have a response.

"How about I get the two of you some of those famous cupcakes that we can all share?" I say, trying to break some of the tension. I get up and head to the counter before anyone has a chance to respond.

When I return with the treats, the ladies are all huddled together. They have all of the bills spread out again. They are trying to figure out a timetable of what bills need to be paid first.

"Before we decide what needs to be paid first," Reggie says, " we need to figure out how much money we have between us. Now that I have put up the money for the funeral upgrades, I don't have a lot left in my savings. *Maybe* five thousand."

"I can probably scrape up about three thousand dollars, at the most," says Bridgid. "But that won't leave me anything to live on… how about you, Tru? Are you in any position to help out?"

"Well, the art world is not very lucrative right now. But I've been doing some temp work on the side, so I might be able to contribute about a thousand—but even that is really pushing it."

"I don't even understand how you can survive in New York as an artist," Reggie says. "You need to find a decent job. I have some connections there, if you want to join the real world."

"That's okay, I don't need any help right now," Trulia says, her expression hardening.

"Well, nine thousand dollars is not going to make it," Reggie says. "We need to think of something. Or else the bank is going to take away the house. Bridgid, why don't you declare bankruptcy for the bakery. That would at least get rid of the bills that are overdue."

"I'm not going to do that to some of the suppliers who have stuck by us all these years," says Bridgid. "And besides, I couldn't do that to our employees. They are like family to me."

"Maybe I can help," I say, interrupting the debate. They all look at me as though they forgot I was there. "I could go through the bills and see if I can work out a payment plan with some of the suppliers."

"Stay out of this Joel," Bridgid yells at me. "Who do you think you are? I don't want you, or anyone else taking over my life."

This outburst stuns me for a second. I have never seen this side of Bridgid. I can't seem to find the right response, that would not embarrass me or Bridgid. So, I get up from the table, back away and head for the door, hoping that I haven't blown things with Bridgid.

bridgid

THE SUN IS HOT AGAINST MY SHOULDERS AND THE STIFF fabric of the funeral dress I wear irritates my skin. I shift uncomfortably as I wait for my sisters to arrive. I am early. Too early but I couldn't just walk around that empty house any longer. I move into the shade of a large willow that towers over the path to the front of the funeral home. It provides some relief from the scorching sun.

My sister's black sedan pulls up to the curb and they climb out, their faces somber. Regina pulls me into a tight hug. I can smell the smoke from the cigarette that she had snuck earlier.

"How are you holding up?" she asks, her own eyes smeared with mascara. I take a shaky breath in.

"I'm doing the best I can. I believe everything is ready if you want to go ahead inside. I just need a few more minutes," I reply, and she grips my hand tightly before leading Katrina into the funeral home. I sag against the rough bark of the willow tree.

I close my eyes and let the wind play across my face. It reminds me of my mother's touch, and I bite back a sob at the unfairness of her death. When I open my eyes, I see that the parking lot is filling with more cars. I trudge up the walkway and into the cool, darkened interior.

My eyes immediately alight on Joel. He smiles as people trail in and presses a program into their hands. He meets my eyes and gives me a small, tentative smile. I return a small smile that does not reach my eyes and his falters before he returns his attention to the line of mourners.

I take my seat next to Katrina near the front. I cannot bring myself to look into the casket, so instead, I stare at my shoes for the entire service. Katrina squeezes my hand when it is time. I lift my eyes and see that the casket has been closed and the ushers lift it to move her to the cemetery. She really is gone. I feel the tears as they course down my face.

I stand next to my sisters as we receive the mourners, but I cannot keep my attention on their remorse. My mind follows my mother down the drive and to the cemetery, her final resting place. "Goodbye, Mama," I whisper and turn back to shake the hand of the next woman in the line.

The rest of the service seems to blur past me. I sit in a corner and twirl my wine glass between my palms. I feel drained. It takes everything I have to not just break down in front of everyone. Thankfully Joel has taken care of every aspect of the ceremony, so I haven't had to do a thing, for which I am grateful.

I know that I need to speak to him. I watch as he flies from person to person and ensures that everything is running smoothly. Feeling embarrassed about my behavior yesterday, a blush climbs my cheeks. I shouldn't have yelled.

Regina sits heavily next to me, causing the chair to buckle a bit. I smell the sweet cloying scent of wine now mingling with a fresh cigarette. She leans her head back against the chair and sighs loudly.

"I'm ready for this to be over," she moans.

"Me too," I say quietly, my eyes still on Joel's broad back. Something stirs deep inside of me, but I push it away.

"He has been great through this," Regina states, her own eyes track Joel as he moves about the room. I cross my arms in front of my chest.

"He has done a good job," I reply tersely.

"He's done more than good," she chides and tips her wineglass back and captures the last drop with a flick of her tongue.

"You should probably talk to him. Yesterday was rather awkward," she says with a groan as she stands.

"I know," I snap. She rolls her eyes at me, the big sister forever irritated by her younger sister.

"Then do it. Haven't you noticed that life is too short?" she retorts and walks away, her hand fumbles in her purse for another cigarette. I watch her back as she walks away, teetering on her spiked heels.

People filter out as they call their goodbyes. I nod, not listening. My heart races as I realize that soon it will just be Joel and I left in the room. I think about leaving but I am frozen in place, absentmindedly toying with my empty wine glass.

Joel moves through the room, collecting the debris, and puts it into a large garbage bag. His eyes dart towards me but he quickly averts his eyes. I take a deep breath and walk over to him as I gather empty plates from the nearby tables. I hold them out to him.

"Thanks," he says with a smile and the heat hits me again as his voice rolls over me. I cannot stop the blush that climbs its way up my face.

"Hey," I reply awkwardly. I realize that I cannot do this here as I fumble for the words. "Can you meet me at the bakery tomorrow? There's something I would like to discuss with you," I say in a hurry. He smiles again and nods once.

"Of course. I can be there around 10 if that works?"

"That is perfect. Thank you." I say and pivot on my heel. I rush from the building, gasping as the bright sunlight burns my eyes but I welcome it after the dimness of the funeral home.

I race to my car and sit behind the wheel as I breathe heavily. I press my forehead against the leather of the steering wheel and let the tears fall freely.

joel

I WATCH HER LEAVE AND IT BREAKS MY HEART.

"Joel?" I startle. Trulia's eyes are red from weeping, but her back is firm and straight. She holds out her hand for a shake. "Thanks, Joel. You made this process way smoother than it might have been."

"Wasn't as smooth as I'd have liked." I smile at her, but I'm still thinking about Bridgid. Despite her perfect, show-stopper body, I did not enjoy watching her walk away from me.

"Don't blame yourself for our mess, Joel. It's not your fault, and there's nothing you can do about it." She sighs. "We'll figure it out like we always do. Anyway, thanks."

She drops my hand and turns toward the open, sunlit door. The words burst out of my mouth before I even realize I'm speaking.

"Tru, wait! I have an idea." She stops and tilts her head at me with a little frown. Was it because I used her nickname? *Man, I'm letting my guard down. Slow up, buddy.*

"I've been thinking that I might be able to help with the money issue." Her eyebrows rise, and she moves closer to me.

"Joel, you don't have to——"

"I know. I know I don't *have* to, but I really want to. Will you hear me out?" She considers, then scans the room for Reggie. Her sister's deep in conversation with a pair of brightly clad elderly women—probably some of Mama's friends.

"Outside," she says. I lead her to the sunlit door, and we step through, heading toward the hundred-year-old willow on the home's front lawn. It offers dappled shade, and more importantly, privacy. "Okay, lemme hear it."

"I want to put together a benefit for Bridgid, to save the bakery."

Tru throws back her head and laughs in a very non-funeral way. The joyful sound rings through the air like a bell.

"Joel!"

"I'm serious."

"No, you don't get me." She shakes her head. "I *know* you're serious. I've known you're serious about Bridgid for a while now."

Uh oh. Did I just give myself away?

"I just want to help—" She stops me, holding up a hand.

"I can see that, and I think it's great." Relief washes over me like cool rain.

"Okay! Here's what I'm thinking." And I lay it out. Tru listens closely, nodding every now and then. Funeral guests continue to trickle out of the home behind us, their shoes crunching on the gravel walkway. I speak quickly, fearing that Reggie could show up at any moment to squash my plans.

"So, let me get this straight." Tru puts her hands on her hips, and glances at the ground, gathering her thoughts. "You want to hold a benefit at the BBQ joint, all proceeds to go toward The Muffin Top."

"Yep."

"And you wanna pull other local businesses into it, too."

"Yep." She purses her lips, closes her eyes briefly.

"This could work…" I open my mouth to reply but she waves me to silence. "But you can't do it alone."

I didn't expect that.

"Why not?" This time, Tru doesn't laugh, but she does grace me with a wide, frank smile.

"Joel, you're a white boy in the black part of town. These business owners don't know you! Why should they trust you, when you're asking them to sacrifice their profits to support a business that *you don't even own*? They're gonna wonder what you're up to."

I hadn't thought of that. *God, I'm an idiot.*

"BUT." Tru gives my shoulder a quick squeeze. "I know your heart's in this for real. So, I'm gonna give you a hand."

"Thank you—"

"Don't you dare thank me. We got work to do." She glances at the funeral home door. Reggie helps one of the brightly dressed women down the two concrete steps to the gravel path. In moments, she'll see us and come over. Tru reaches into her funky, patchwork handbag and pulls out her phone.

"What's your number?"

I tell her, and she punches it in. Then she slides the phone back into the bag and hitches it over her shoulder.

"Give me two hours, then meet me outside the Bakery."

"What are we gonna do?"

Tru smiles again.

"You ever hear of the Belton Network?" She asks.

"The what?" She chuckles.

"No, I guess you wouldn't have. It's the most efficient and trusted way to spread information in the black community. In fact——" She points to the elderly woman that Reggie helped down the steps, now making her way carefully along the gravel path toward the parking lot. "Miss Helen runs the Network. So, we're gonna ask for her advice."

"Let's talk to her now." I turn toward Miss Helen, but Tru grabs my elbow.

"Hold on, Joel, that's not how it's done." Now I see Reggie notice us from the funeral home door. She starts down the steps. Trulia drops her voice to a whisper.

"Two hours, outside the Bakery. And bring something for Miss Helen." Reggie's on the gravel path now, coming on fast.

"Like what?" I hiss between my teeth.

"Sweets, perfume, flowers, something *nice*." Tru locks eyes with me to make sure I've got it. I don't, but we're out of time. She lifts her face to Reggie, who offers a distracted smile to me and takes Trulia's arm. They head toward the parking lot.

Tru doesn't look back as I stand rooted to the spot. *Something nice for Miss Helen? What the heck does that mean?*

"Joel?" Addie, one of our Attendants, leans out of the funeral home door. "The family doesn't want the flowers. Shall I take them to the nursing home?" I nod my head, grateful for the distraction.

"As always, Addie. Hope you don't mind the trip." Addie laughs, a soft, hiccupping sound.

"Never on your life. Love the old dears. Gonna be one myself someday." She disappears inside.

I'll join her and close the place up. Then, I'll do a bit of desperation shopping for that "something nice."

God help me.

Chapter Thirty-Three

bridgid

It's only ten a.m., and I'm already a ball of stress.

Why was I such a bitch to Joel? Of course, I'm missing Mama real bad. But come on, girl!

I wipe the counter furiously, as if erasing every ugly word I shouted at him. I need a break, but the bakery is so busy this morning that I'm buzzing around like a caffeinated bee. If one more person asks me to make a latte…

"Annette! Can you bring more lemon poppyseed? We're almost out."

"I'll be there in a second, *okay?*" She sounds stressed, too. I hear the clang of baking trays.

What's she doing back there?

"Oh no, the brownies!" I forgot all about them. I whirl around to rush to the oven and run straight into Annette. The basket she carries pops out of her hand, and muffins fly from it in all directions.

"Whoa! I'm sorry, oh god, I'm so sorry!" Her wide blue eyes fill with tears.

Suddenly I just can't take it anymore. I grab her arm and pin her against the counter.

"Annette Stevens, don't you cry. You hear me? Do! Not! Cry! If you cry—*if you cry*—you're FIRED!"

The Bakery goes still. Customers pause mid-bite to watch. We stand frozen nose to nose, breathing hard, my angry face glaring into her scared face.

Then, we burst out laughing.

Great, shrieking, sloppy laughs that bounce off the walls like those unhappy muffins. We collapse against each other and laugh until we choke. The customers start chuckling, too, and then, they applaud!

"Bridgid?" Annette and I look up from where we've crumpled to the ground. We see nothing but a pair of eyes and the top of a blond head peering over the counter.

That sets us off again. We wail and snort until our ribs ache.

"Are you all right?"

"Joel…. I'm fine…" I wipe my face with my apron. "We had an accident."

"A muffin accident," Annette says.

"It was tragic."

"Totally tragic," she says.

"What?" Joel says.

And that sets us off again.

"Sorry, sorry, Joel! Annette, will you go check on those brownies? They're probably charcoal by now." I help her stand, and she gathers her basket, and stumbles back to the kitchen.

"Rough morning?" Joel still looks confused. I don't blame him.

"Let's step outside for a sec."

I hadn't noticed before, but the morning air feels fresh and sharp. I lead Joel across the street to a bench in the sun. He sits beside me, and we gaze at the Bakery. I can't quite look at him yet.

"Mama loved this place," I say.

"She surely did."

Somehow, mentioning Mama makes me brave. I turn to him.

"Joel, I owe you an apology—"

"Nope." That pulls me up short.

"What?"

"I don't want your lousy apology." His smile, warm and crooked, makes me smile.

"Well, I want to give it to you. I was a jerk the other day. I felt guilty about Mama's finances, and helpless to fix the problem, and I just… I don't know…"

"Mad at the world?"

"Mad at the world. And I took it out on you. I am so sorry." I watch his eyes soften from careful to something else. Tender?

"You're going through a really rough time right now. You're allowed."

We return to watching customers move in and out of the Bakery. Then, Joel clears his throat, and sits up straighter on the bench.

"I've got something to say. Will you promise to listen until I'm done?"

"Okay…"

"Here goes." He takes a deep breath. The fact that he's nervous makes *me* nervous. "Your sister Trulia and I have arranged a fund-raiser. For you. For the bakery."

If you asked me to describe the last thing in the world I expected Joel to say, that would be it.

"What—"

"You promised!" He gives me a sharp look, and I press my lips together. "Billy Bob's barbeque joint will lead the effort. This weekend, they'll set aside all their proceeds to save the Bakery. And I mean ALL their proceeds. Even from their biggest nights of the week, Friday and Saturday, when they're so busy they can't keep up with the orders."

My breath accelerates.

"But that's not all. Next week, they're gonna add items from the Bakery to their dessert menu. They do way more volume than the Bakery does. All of that money will go to the Bakery, too."

I feel dizzy. *This can't be happening.*

"With the help of some influential parties," Joel pauses and actually *winks* at me. "We also got a bunch of local businesses to donate auction items, stuff like fancy meals, wine, jewelry, you name it. The auction will happen in a couple weeks, and that money's coming to you, too."

Streams of tears course down my cheeks. It takes me a second to realize I'm weeping.

"Finally—"

"There's *more?*" He holds up a finger to quiet me.

"Finally, some of Hibbert's clients want to pitch in. One person is donating space for the auction, another is making arrangements with First State Bank to pay three months of Muffin Tops' rent…" Joel looks up at the sky and shakes his head.

"Bridgid, people loved and respected your Mama, and they think the world of you, too. They're falling all over themselves to help you out." He falls silent.

We just sit for a minute. Just two people on a park bench. It strikes me that the folks passing by have no idea what's happening here.

"Are you saying…" I don't trust my voice.

"Go on."

"Are you saying that it's gonna be okay?" The dimple on the left side of his face deepens. It's the most beautiful thing I've ever seen.

"Yep. I guess that's what I'm saying."

I shriek and throw my arms around his neck. He grunts in surprise and we nearly tumble off the bench. Then I pull back, grab his face in both hands, and give him the hottest, deepest, longest kiss ever.

And I don't give a damn who sees.

bridgid

JOEL'S HAND FUMBLES FOR THE DOORKNOB AS I PRESS UP against him, our mouths engaged in a passionate kiss. His exhalations fill my mouth, carrying a tang of the coffee he had with breakfast. I can feel his growing bulge pressing hard into me.

He gets the door open at last and we surge into the office. I kick back with my heel and shut the door as I sweep my fingers through his soft hair.

"Bridgid," he gasps, chest heaving with heavy swells. Joel's eyes smolder with molten desire. "Oh, Bridgid…"

His mouth goes to my neck, kissing softly. A moan flies from my wide-open mouth as we barrel back into the desk. Joel grabs me around my waist, lifting me into the air to settle me on top of the desk. I feel a paperclip or something under my butt, but I'm far too distracted to care.

I want him so bad. I want him *now.* I grab the bulge in his crotch, cooing as I flash a smile up at him.

That's all the encouragement Joel needs. He hikes up my skirt around my waist, his fingers trembling with desperate need. Joel hooks his fingers in the waistband of my panties and drags them down to my knees, then my ankles, and finally all the way off.

I gasp as he shoves my thighs apart. Joel trails kisses along my inner thigh, raising goosebumps on my sensitive skin. His warm breath tingles across my pussy as he moves his mouth in close.

"Joel," I gasp. "You're a bad boy, Joel…"

My mouth flies open as his tongue works its way through my wet gash. I grasp the sides of his head, pressing him into me as he grows bolder with his oral explorations. Joel envelops one of my labia in his mouth, suckling like a greedy calf. My eyes squeeze shut as a long, desperate groan forces its way from my throat.

"That feels so good," I manage to gasp. Joel brings his long, slender fingers into play, prying my pussy open and worming their way inside. He moves over to the opposite labia as I ease back onto the desk, until I'm lying flat with my legs in the air draped over his broad shoulders.

Joel swishes his fingers about inside of me, working me into a frenzy. He stretches my labia out with his mouth, sucking like mad. Joel releases my swollen pussy lip and moves up. When his hot breath blows over my clit, I let out a pleading whimper.

"Oh yes," I gasp. "Yes, please."

Joel swishes his tongue in slow circles around my clitoral mound, not quite touching my little lady. One hand busies itself with fingers thrusting slow like a cock, while the other moves up to pinch a nipple through my shirt. I cry out, grabbing his wrist but making no attempt to stop him.

Joel kisses my clit carefully and I melt into the desk. He lifts his mouth from my body for a moment.

"Your pussy tastes so good, Bridgid."

Then he wraps his lips around my clit and sucks. All the while his fingers slide in and out, in and out. I let out a sharp cry, unmindful of who might hear it.

"I'm coming," I gasp. "I'm *coming*!"

Fireworks explode behind my eyelids as I climax. A tremor of pleasure throbs from my crotch to spread to every nerve ending. I float on a golden cloud as Joel lifts me aloft on the wings of ecstasy.

My cunny squirts out hot juice into his face, but Joel doesn't seem to mind. He laps it up eagerly, then lifts his glistening face to stare into my eyes.

With one hand still messing around with my cunny, he unbuckles his belt with the other. Joel fumbles his rigid cock into view. I swoon at the contrast between us, his pale flesh against my dark mocha skin. Joel extracts his fingers and uses the dripping wet digits to spread my lips wide open.

"I've wanted to fuck all day," Joel groans. He shoves the head of his throbbing member inside of me. I arch my back, easing his ingress into my quivering love tunnel. Joel stretches me, filling me up with his thick slab until it goes all the way in. I cry out sharply when he thrusts the first time.

Joel grabs my hips and leans into the thrusts, bending my legs upward. I rear back against the desk, my chest heaving with heavy pants. His eyes blaze with desire, focused squarely on me. I feel as if I might be immolated by that smoldering gaze, and I look forward to my annihilation.

My cries grow sharper, higher in pitch as he drives his sweating body into my own. His balls slap into my anus, triggering sensations there which spread into my cunny and then throughout the rest of my body. I reach up and squeeze his chest, feeling the firm knots of muscle under my fingers. Joel grimaces a bit when my nails dig in, but he doesn't falter one iota.

"Oh Joel," I cry. "Harder, Joel. Harder, please."

Joel slaps his palms down on either side of my body, knocking a heavy metal stapler to the floor with a clunk. He blinks sweat out of his eyes as he drives his cock into me harder. I throw my head back and moan.

"Yes, yes, oh god, that's perfect——"

I feel myself inching toward the precipice of a truly monumental climax. My eyes water as he thrusts into me, triggering every nerve into fiery wakefulness. I slip over the edge and my body writhes like a worm on a hot summer sidewalk beneath his comforting bulk. A scream pierces the air, and it takes me a moment to realize it's my own.

I fly away on the wings of climax, feeling almost as if I'm floating above it all, yet still connected by fiery tendrils to my corporeal form. Joel collapses on top of me, sweeping me into his embrace. He hugs me tightly, drawing me into a sitting position while his cock remains buried inside of me.

"Bridgid," he whispers in my ear. I hold him close, feeling fulfilled and happy for the first time in what seems like forever.

Chapter Thirty-Five

bridgid

I STOOD ON MY TIP TOES, TRYING TO REACH THE CAN OF Clabber Girl baking powder on the top shelf of the Muffin Top's pantry.

"Come on," I grunt, straining my fingers to the utmost. "Come on."

My index finger bumps the can, knocking it over on its side. Thanks to the slight unevenness of the shelf, it rolls down the grade out of sight.

"Stupid can." I settle back onto the flats of my feet and glance around the kitchen. Regina stands pert and proper in her white apron, using a butter knife to level off a cup of flour to razor sharp exactness. I don't see Joel anywhere.

"Regina, do you happen to know where Joel got himself off to?"

Regina's eyes narrow as she carefully pours the cup of flour into the shiny metal mixing bowl. She dusts off her hands and turns to face me.

"Wasn't he just here?"

"I thought so, too, but I know now he's disappeared." I sigh and stare up at the shelf. Sometimes I really hate being short.

"Is there something I can do to help?"

I glance over at Regina and chuckle.

"Not unless you can grow another foot." I point up at the shelf containing the toppled Clabber Girl baking powder. "Our last can of Clabber Girl decided to roll away from me."

"I told Mama for years to fix that shelf." Regina sighs. "I'll go look for him."

"Go look for who?"

Joel sweeps into the kitchen, arms laden with brown paper grocery bags. He settles them on the prep table with a rustle, the tendons flexing in his forearms.

"You." I flash him a quick smile. Memories of our tryst in the office spring back into my mind. I can tell he thought about it, too, from the way a slight pinkness came to his cheeks. "I need a tall person."

"And a tall person you shall receive."

I point up at the shelf. "Can you reach the can of baking powder up there?"

"No problem." Joel leans up against the shelves and feels around blindly. I hear a thump, and then he drags the can out into view. "Here you go. This is an industrial sized can. I thought it was coffee at first."

"We go through it pretty quick." I check the date on the top of the can and sigh in relief. If you use stale baking powder, nothing will rise properly—and nobody wants to buy flat muffins.

I take the can from his hands and set it on the prep table. "Hey, what are you up to after this, Joel?"

He chuckles softly. "I'm up to whatever you tell me to do?"

I pinch his cheek, enjoying the way his skin pinks. "Right answer."

Joel gives me a quick peck on the lips. "I figure things out, eventually."

"Ugh, get a room," Reggie mutters, rolling her eyes. "Or sneak off to the office again."

I cover my mouth with my hand, eyes going wide as I exchange glances with Joel. He kind of shrugs. I'd thought we were more discreet than we obviously had been.

An alarm goes off, and I rush over towards the oven, slipping on black silicone mitts as I go. I open the oven door, feeling a rush of heat blowing into my face, carrying with it a whiff of cranberry orange muffins. I grin in satisfaction at the perfectly golden brown, puffy tops.

"Here we go," I say, putting the tins on the cooling racks. I stare at the assembly line we have set up. The baked goods go from the oven to the cooling racks, then to a station where they are carefully scooped or removed from their tins, then to a second cooling station under the rapidly swishing ceiling fan. Finally, one of our trio—whichever one isn't busy with something else at the moment—takes the last step of wrapping them in plastic and affixing the price tag.

I stare at the big pile of goods already done and do a quick estimate in my head. I feel a surge of despair when I realize that we're only halfway finished. If we're going to pull this bake sale off, we're going to need an enormous amount of goods.

Without Joel and Regina's help, there's no way I could pull this off. I pop over to where Regina is taking chocolate chips one by one and plopping them into a measuring cup.

"Regina, what are you doing—are you seriously counting the chocolate chips individually? Just pour in two cups like the recipe says."

"Sure, I could do that. I could just grab a handful of flour and throw it in like Gram used to as well. Who cares if it comes out dry? Or someone gets a cookie without sufficient chips?"

I hold my hands in the air in surrender. "Never mind. I'll leave you to it, then."

The doorbell rings. I glance up in confusion. Our sign clearly says we're closed.

"Who could it be now?"

"Let them stand around like a damn fool until they learn how to read," Regina quips.

Joel's eyes widen. "Oh, that's probably the reporter from the Telegram."

"Reporter?" Regina and I exchange glances. "What reporter?"

"I know people say print is dead," Joel says as he rinses the flour off his hands in the sink rapidly "but around these parts, people still read the daily newspaper. It skews right to our target demographic. The same folks who love bake sales have newspaper subscriptions."

"Make sure you show him the graphics Trulia came up with," Regina calls as he sweeps out of the kitchen.

Joel returns a moment later with an older white man with a nimbus of gray hair around his shiny dome. He introduces himself as Kyle Reilly. His nostrils flare as he inhales deeply.

"It smells positively wonderful in here, y'all." He licks his lips as he stares at the muffins recently removed from the oven. "What kind are those, if you don't mind my asking?"

I grin and put one of the muffins on a little paper plate, then hand it over to him.

"Orange cranberry. Old family recipe."

Kyle bites into the muffin and his eyes flutter closed. "Mmmm! Wow, if all your stuff is this good, I might just buy the entire batch myself."

I exchange excited glances with Joel. It's really coming together. I have a good feeling about this bake sale.

Maybe we can save Mama's house after all.

joel

THE AIR SEEMS ELECTRIC WITH PROMISE AS I THROW THE van doors open and extract my first load of baked goods. The plastic shines with the hot Texas sun as I carry them through the back door of Billy Bob's BBQ, careful not to dislodge the mop handle which holds the portal open for my ingress.

Behind me, Bridgid trudges along under the weight of the fondue pot. Trulia had the idea of dipping marshmallows in the chocolate morass so we could have at least one hot, ready to eat item on our smorgasbord of sweet confections.

I smile at the kitchen staff as they make way for us. The smell of brown sugar and molasses set my belly rumbling. There's time enough for lunch later... for now, it's time for some good old-fashioned hard labor. I sweep through the kitchen into the dining area. The staff of Billy Bob's have shoved two long, wooden tables together near the rear wall, and set up several white plastic folding numbers as well.

I do a quick estimate and grin. There should be more than enough space for all of our goods. I settle my burden down and turn toward Bridgid, reaching out for the fondue pot. She drags it back, cocking an eyebrow at me.

"Aren't you forgetting something?"

I grin and lean over, pecking her on the lips as I remove the fondue pot from her arms. I turn about and place it on the table as an elderly man from a nearby table grins.

"Is this the bake sale I read about in the paper?" he asks in a thin, reedy voice.

I turn and smile at him. "Indeed, it is…"

I realize I recognize this man. I tended to his cousin several months ago at the mortuary.

"…Mr. Kelling."

Kelling smiles widely. "Ah, you remember. I just wanted to thank you for the way you comforted my sister during the wake. She spoke very highly of you."

"It's what I do," I say with a shrug. "Excuse me a second, Mr. Kelling, but I have more stuff to unload."

"Don't mind me. I'll just be sitting here, staring longingly at those Orange Cranberry muffins."

"You get a discount if you buy a baker's dozen," I say with a wink as I sweep back into the kitchen. I nearly collide with Regina as she staggers in under a too-heavy load of brownies in wicker baskets.

"Watch it," she snaps, moving her body to the side to squeeze past me.

"Sorry." I dash back out the rear door and find Bridgid has crawled into the van, her well-rounded bottom the only thing visible. She glances over her shoulder and cocks an angular eyebrow.

"Are you checking out my ass, Joel?"

"Yes," I admit.

"Right answer." She gives it a little wriggle and we both laugh. Bridgid drags out a big tray of lime green divinity, brown bits of walnut furrowing the surface here and there. As she hands it to me, a sigh heaves from her full lips.

"What's wrong?"

"I'm anxious, is all. We're going to have to sell pretty much every single thing in the van if we want to save Mama's house."

"No need to be anxious." I peck her on the forehead as I take the tray of divinity. "It'll be fine. How big of pieces should I put on plates?"

She frowns down at the confection in the tray. "A good-sized chunk. Enough that it doesn't look small compared to the plate. You got the tiny ones, right?"

"Yeah. Fancy ones, with bumblebee art along the borders."

"Joel, you shouldn't be spending your own money on this."

I grinned. "No worries. I get the stuff at a bulk discount. Jeff Bezos has probably added a new addition to his mansion just based on how much paper product I move for him."

I carry the divinity into the restaurant floor and set it on the table. Using a plastic knife—so I won't damage Bridgid's high end cookie sheet—I cut it into three-inch squares. I then lift each piece up and gently lay it on a plate. Trulia wraps each plate in green saran wrap and then adds a price tag.

"Three dollars for a piece of divinity?" I ask, cocking an eyebrow.

Trulia puts her hands on her hips and glares at me. "Have you ever had my sister's divinity before?"

"No."

She uses the knife to sever a wedge the size of her finger and lifts it up toward my mouth. I place my palm under the knife in case it falls and gently pick it off. I pop the dollop of green confection into my mouth. Sweet flavor explodes on my tongue, with just a hint of spice.

"Wow," I say around the masticated mouthful. "Okay, we're probably lowballing it."

"Told you."

It takes over an hour to fully set up the bake sale. Trulia's gorgeous banners ripple in the air from the AC vent, adding to the festive air. The Billy Bob's staff bring us a pitcher of tart pink lemonade, which goes down in a matter of minutes. I hadn't expected to work up so much of a sweat.

"One last detail." I squeeze Bridgid's shoulder as I move past her and return to the van. I extract the heavy plastic cash register, the cord dangling down to thump against my leg as I carry it inside the restaurant.

We have to bum an extension cord to reach the outlet, but when the green lights flash into view a grin stretches over my lips.

"Are you folks open for business, now?" Mr. Kelling asks hopefully.

"We are officially open for business, sir," Bridgid says with a grin.

"Great. I'll take a dozen of your Orange Cranberry Muffins."

Bridgid rings him up. "That'll be seventeen dollars and thirty-eight cents, sir."

"Here you go," Mr. Kelling says, handing her a fifty. Bridgid frowns.

"I'm not sure I have enough cash to give you change for this yet. Do you have anything smaller?"

"Keep the change," Mr. Kelling says with a wink. "I'd hate to see your Mama's house leave the family. They might move a Yankee into the neighborhood."

We share a laugh as he shuffles off with his prize.

"Well, this is an auspicious start," I offer.

Bridgid grins up at me with cautious optimism glittering in her brown eyes. I have a feeling it's going to be a good day.

Chapter Thirty-Seven

bridgid

Early in the afternoon, the bake sale really gets going as people get off work and/or school. Thanks to the nearby Mary Hardin Baylor university, we get a whole flood of college kids homesick for some good old-fashioned baked goods.

The cash drawer becomes so stuffed full of money that I have to bag it up in a zipping, locking bank bag and hand it off to Joel. He locks it in the van for safe keeping and returns to help the ever-expanding line.

It seems like everyone in Belton has turned out for the bake sale. While not everyone is quite as generous as Mr. Kelling, most folks don't ask for their change back. Sweat glistens on my brow as I ring up sale after sale.

The divinity turned out to be such a hit I find myself wishing I'd baked a few extra trays. I catch Joel stashing some of it away for himself and chuckle. Well, he's certainly earned it.

"Excuse me," says one rail thin blonde woman with a pinched face. "Do you have any gluten-free options?"

"As a matter of fact, I do." I point over at the third plastic table. "Everything wrapped in blue is gluten-free."

Her face beams with a smile. "Well, that's great! You wouldn't believe how many people ignore us. Did you use vegan flour?"

I keep a smile plastered on my face as I think *All flour is vegan, you moron.*

"Of course, ma'am. You might say I never use anything else."

Regina snaps a glare in my direction as Gluten Free Lady saunters over to the blue wrapped bundles.

"Do you *have* to chat up every single person? We're on a time limit here. Seeds of Soul are going to set up a performance at seven PM and it's going on five!"

"Don't worry, I think we're going to run out of product long before then," I say, looking at the rapidly diminishing stores. "Besides, every person who comes in here is a potential customer for Muffin Top. For life. I'm not chatting people up. I'm growing our brand."

Regina's eyes widen. Her lips twitch a rare smile. "Well played, Bridgid. Well played."

Joel comes over and peers into the cash tray. "Do I need to make another run to the van?"

I glance down at the over-stuffed trays. "I think so. Just leave me enough to make change with. I never thought we'd get this kind of turn out."

"We did a full-on media blitz," Joel says with a chuckle as he gathers the bills into another blue bank envelope. "If there's one thing that goes over in small town Texas it's— well, it's probably football, but bake sales are a close second. Thanks to Reilly's article, the whole town knew to come out."

I smile at him as he moves to carry the cash out to the van. I grasp his wrist and drag him back.

"What?" He asks when he sees my somber expression.

"Joel, I…" I swallow hard and lick my lips nervously. "I just…thank you. For everything."

He smiles wider. "It was my pleasure."

Joel goes to leave, but I hang on to his wrist. He turns back to me, cocking an eyebrow.

"What is it?"

"Joel, I think I love you."

My heart hammers in my chest. There, I said it. I feel simultaneously freed and anxious as I await his response.

Joel's eyes soften. He places his hand on my cheek and I sigh.

"I love you, too, Bridgid." He kisses my forehead. "I'll be right back."

Reluctantly, I let go of his wrist. I turn back around to my sisters. Trulia's hands are clasped over her mouth, her eyes as wide as dinner plates. Regina turns her face away, sniffling as she wipes at her eyes.

"Regina, are you…are you crying?"

"No. Shut up." She dabs at her face. "I just got some dust in my eyes or something. Mind your business!"

"She is crying," Tru says happily. "Oh, Bridgid, Joel's so sweet. You two are perfect for each other! I'm so happy for you."

"I can't get over the fact Regina's icy exterior is melting," I say, shaking my head.

"Don't you have muffins to sell?" Reggie snaps, taking off her gloves and rushing to the bathroom. "I have to pee."

Trulia and I hug, and then return to serving hungry customers. The dinner crowd is bleeding through the door, and every one of them eyes our bake sale for potential dessert. I'm a little surprised we have so many chocolate chip cookies left, to be honest. I'd have thought they'd be gone quick.

"Oh boy," Joel says, rushing back to the table. "Get ready for a deluge. A Little League team is on their way inside!"

I rub my hands together eagerly. "All right! Time to put this bake sale to bed. And just in time, too!"

I notice a tall, lanky and handsome man carrying in a guitar and an amplifier. Must be the Seeds of Soul guys getting ready for their set.

The Little League team cleans us out. Especially the fathers, who evaporate our chocolate chip cookie supply in a matter of minutes.

We clean up after our sale before counting the money. I'm brimming with anxiety. Did we make enough? My happiness at Joel and I confessing our love is tampered with worry. Will we be able to save Mama's house after all?

I sit in the back of the now-empty van, tallying up our funds. I lay one stack of rubber-band bound ones on top of the growing pile and tap on the adding machine. With a mechanical whirr, the receipt grows longer and longer.

"What are we looking at?" Joel asks eagerly as I stare at the grand total.

I flop onto my back and stare at the ceiling of the van. Joel crouches down beside me, concern writ large on his face.

"Bridgid? What's wrong?"

A wide grin spreads over my face. "Nothing. Nothing's wrong! We have enough."

I burst into a girlish giggle.

"We have enough!"

Joel hugs me tight as Trulia and Regina whoop with delight.

joel

I PULL UP OUTSIDE OF BRIDGID'S MOTHER'S HOUSE—NOW hers—just as the sun kisses the horizon with red-gold light. Peering intently at my reflection in the vanity mirror, I smooth back a few stray hairs and bare my teeth for inspection. No bits stuck between my teeth. I do a sniff check of my armpits and found them more akin to Dove Men Total Care instead of pungent sweat.

Why am I so nervous?

I give it some thought and realize it's because this will be the first night we've spent together since our confession at the bake sale. I guess that puts some pressure on me. I don't know why—everything has worked out splendidly.

My boots crunch the gravel as I make my way up the driveway. I see a figure staring out one of the windows, then a few seconds later the front door opens.

"Hey there," Bridgid says, standing framed in the doorway. "Aren't you a long, cool drink of water?"

My mouth gapes open. Her hair has been pulled back into a tight bun, spare length dangling over her shoulder like forest vines. Bridgid's full lips bear a smear of brick red gloss, her eyes glittering with purple eyeshadow. It's her outfit that really takes me by surprise, however.

She's wearing---she's not wearing very much, that's for sure. I run my eyes up her body starting with her shiny black heels, then on to her stocking-clad, shapely legs. The stockings are held in place by red lace garters dangling from a matching belt around her slim waist. A tiny triangle of scarlet shields her loins from my view, a shelf bra pushes her generous breasts up into view. Her nipples harden right before my eyes as I continue to sweep my gaze upward.

"Like what you see?" Bridgid swings the door open wide and turns her back to me. I take in the sight of her lovely, dark-skinned form. I've seen more cotton in the top of an aspirin bottle than in her panties. Mesmerized by the way her bared cheeks dance, I follow her up the steps to the bedroom.

Bridgid crawls onto the bed, swinging her hips sensuously as she goes. I follow as if in a trance, my cock growing stiff and straining at my jeans.

"Is that for me?" she asks. At first, I think she means my rod, but then I look down and realize I'm still holding a bouquet of flowers in my hand.

"Yes," I say, voice breaking. Bridgid's eyes twinkle with delight.

"Set them down on the nightstand," she purrs. "There'll be plenty of time to find a vase later."

I set the flowers down and turn around to find her up on her knees, a finger inside her mouth. I move onto the bed, taking her into my arms. I mash my mouth on those perfect lips, exulting in the feel of their plumpness against my skin.

"I love you," I murmur into her neck as I trail tender kisses.

"I love you, too." Bridgid's nails scrape my belly as she lifts my shirt hem up. I lift my arms in the air so she can pull it off. She bites her lower lip as she runs her hands over my chest. "Goddamn, you are one jacked mortician."

I sweep my hands down her back, tracing over the lace of her bra, down past the garter belt, until I encompass her sweet cheeks in my palms. I grip them tightly, kneading the pliant flesh in my hands. Bridgid moans softly, leaving kisses on my chest.

Her hands busy themselves with my belt, yanking it off with a quick snap. She loops the end over the back of my head and drags me down on top of her. We kiss deeply as the belt slips away. I cup her breast and trace a finger around her swollen nub in the center.

I kiss my way down her neck, across her sternum over to her nipple. I breath hot and heavy over her skin, then run my tongue across her areola in little circles. I flick my tongue over her nipple, and she gasps, clutching the back of my head and drawing me more tightly against her.

"Bridgid," I murmur into her flesh. "I need you so bad."

"I'm all yours, Joel," she sighs. "I'm all yours…"

She tugs down my underwear and I kick out of them. I play with her underwear and find a convenient snap fastening. I rear up enough to look into her rich umber gaze as I snap it loose. Bridgid gasps, her chest heaving as I yank her panties away from her body. The smell of her deeply aroused snatch intensifies, filing my senses with a heady rush. I run my hands along her silken clad thighs, gently spreading them wide.

I slide down until I mash my face into her glistening wet snatch. I exult in her scent, in the feel of her petal soft, swollen labia caressing my skin. Her clitoris swells, quivering, pink, inviting.

I pinch her clitoris firmly as I flick my tongue through her gash. Bridgid's sharp cry echoes off the painted walls.

The dying sun casts a gentle glow over her magnificent mocha skin. I spread her cunny wide open, enjoying the contrast of brown and pink as I slip my tongue inside.

Keeping her clitoris pinched, I slather it with my tongue. Bridgid's grip in my hair tightens until I think she's going to tear it out by the root. Not that I care. I'm so given over to my own desire for her that I don't think I'd notice if someone dropped a truck on me.

I devour her pussy with gusto, giving lots of attention to clitoris but not leaving out her swollen pussy lips. Bridgid's cries grow sharper, closer together as she writhes under my ministrations. She arches her back, thrusting her crotch into me more firmly as I suckle her clitty like there's no tomorrow.

Bridgid's cry of climax heralds a sudden deluge dousing me with her pussy juice. I swallow her sweetness, intoxicated by her intense reaction.

I straighten up, staring down at her gyrating body. Bridgid's eyes flutter open. She looks down between my legs at the rock-solid erection throbbing there.

Wordlessly, she spreads her legs wider and pries her pussy open. I grip my shaft and move in for the kill.

Chapter Thirty-Nine

bridgid

FLASHES OF ELECTRIC DELIGHT STILL PULSE THROUGH MY body as Joel stares down at me with desire writ large on his glistening face. I squirted all over him, again. Some guys are grossed out by that. Not Joel. He acts like he's been anointed with holy water.

Joel runs the swollen head of his cock through my slit. A hiss escapes my throat as I bask in his attention. Tingles emanate from my clit and spread through my entire body, filling me with electric anticipation.

I rear up and grasp his shaft, intending to push him inside of me. Joel grins and pushes me back onto the bed firmly. I titter with soft laughter as he returns to teasing me with his cock.

"You want this?" he asks, sliding the swollen crown over my clit and making me cry out.

"Yes," I purr. "Give it to me."

"Only if you're a good girl."

I chuckle gently, then rear up and get my knees under me. He wants me to be a good girl? Screw that. I'm going to show him how much bad girls need love, too.

I grasp his shaft firmly in my hand, the brown enveloping the paler peach. My painted nails sparkle in the fading sunlight as I slide my hand along his rod. I enjoy the feel of his big, pulsing vein against my palm.

I keep eye contact with him as I open my mouth and run my tongue along the underside of his crown. Joel's mouth flies open, his eyes squeeze shut as I ply my tongue all along his sensitive flesh. A gobbet of precum glistens pearlescent in the gentle evening light. I wait until he opens my eyes so he can watch me greedily lick it clean.

I cradle his balls in my hand, fondling them while I take just the tip inside my mouth. I make plenty of coos and sighs to let him know how much fun I'm having. Joel's hand goes to the back of my head as I take more of his length inside.

Inch by inch, I gobble up his pulsing shaft until his balls rest under my chin. His crown hits the back of my throat, making me gag slightly. I come off his rod, a bit of cum dripping from my lips, before going back down on him.

"Oh, Bridgid," he gasps. "You're so beautiful."

I'll just bet I am. How can a lap full of hair not be beautiful? I feel him grow hard as a rock inside of my mouth. His body draws tight as a bowstring, and he gently taps the top of my head.

"Here it comes," he gasps.

Aww, how sweet. He's giving me a chance to get off his dick before he spews in my mouth. Too bad I have no problem drinking Joel's cum. I love every inch of him, pun intended.

I accept the hot gush in my mouth, drinking it in while rolling my eyes up to meet his gaze. Joel looks at me in shock, as if I'm a revelation. I drag myself off of him and lick a stray drop from his member, smiling up at him and blinking my eyes prettily.

"That's right, baby," I coo. "You hit the jackpot."

Joel's handsome face crinkles with a smile. "Now I'm about to hit something else."

He eases me onto my back, crawling naked on top of me. Our skin slides together. The hairs on his chest feathery soft against me. Joel kisses me deeply, his tongue lashing against my own inside my mouth. He pulls up to his knees and grabs his shaft.

This time he doesn't bother with a tease. He slides his cock between my wide open, dripping wet pussy lips. I moan sharply as he glides into me deeply. I grasp his chest, raking my nails down his skin as he thrusts the first time. The bed rocks, headboard cracking against the wall as he drives his hips into me.

My mouth flies open with a sharp cry. Stars flash behind my eyelids as he pushes me into a climax, and he's just getting started. The steady rhythmic crack of the headboard mingles with our bodies colliding, and the sounds of my increasingly high tempo groans and moans.

"Oh God, Joel," I gasp. "I feel so full…"

Joel grabs my wrists, prying my hands from his chest. I've left angry red lines down his skin. He shoves my hands down to the bed and pounds away, blinking sweat out of his eyes. There's a moment when he gives himself over fully to his desire, where I am his entire world. In that moment I come harder than I ever have in my entire life.

I wrap my legs around his torso, locking my ankles at the small of his back. Joel grins through his desire, his body straining against my own. We're locked in a grapple, battling for the ultimate rush as we seek to drive our pleasure ever higher.

My cries reverberate off the walls as he thrusts his cock in and out, in and out. I grind my pelvis into him, giving him permission for the release he's been so desperate to hold back. We come together, his passionate yowl mingling with my high-pitched scream.

Joel collapses on top of me as I'm flying on a sublime cloud of bliss. Our sweat cools and mingles as I kick my heels off to clop heavily onto the floor.

We wind up laying on our sides, him spooning me from behind. I rest my cheek on his bicep, feeling totally relaxed and cared for in his warm embrace. I snuggle up to him and sigh in contentment.

"I love you, Bridgid," he whispers in my ear.

"I love you, Joel." I caress his forearm before weaving my fingers with his. We lay there as the sun gives up its last gasp and drops from sight, plunging the Texas hills into gentle darkness.

joel

I STROLL OUT TO MY CAR IN THE MORTUARY PARKING LOT, an extra bounce in my step. I greet the late afternoon sun with a cheerful smile. With a pat to the bulge in my pocket, I leap into my car and head for home.

The slowest senior citizen driver ahead of me, and the fastest tailgater on my bumper can't ruin my good mood. Not today. Even when a bird leaves a white, streaking present along the windshield I smile. I just hit the wipers and sluice it away with a spurt of azure fluid.

I can't wait to get back to Bridgid. By now, she should have the bakery locked up for the night and be home. I try to remember which of us was supposed to cook tonight and come to the conclusion it was mine. At a red light I send off an order to our favorite delivery, Fajita Kings, and then trundle on home.

I step out of the car and crunch my way up the gravel to the front door. I'm pleased to see her car in the driveway as well. My fingers close around the knob and twist the spindle, popping the door open.

"Honey, I'm home."

Bridgid stares up at me from the sofa, tucking something behind her back as I enter. I cock an eyebrow but I'm too excited to call her on it.

"I've got something to tell you," we both say at the same time. After a hearty laugh, she unfolds from the sofa and comes into my waiting arms.

"You go first," I say, kissing her tenderly.

"No, you," she says.

I tilt my head to the side.

"Ladies first."

"Sheeeit, I don't see how you can call me a lady after all we did last night."

I chuckle and smooth my hand down her sinuous back. "It's nothing compared to what we're going to do tonight…well, maybe."

"Maybe?" She arched a brow. "Are you tired? Need a night off?"

She playfully pokes me in the belly until I giggle like a schoolboy.

"I'm not tired—"

"You better not be. Just chug a Red Bull, because I decide when you get a night off."

"Who says I even want one?"

She smiles, and I kiss her lips again. Bridgid melts into me. I run my hand down and grab a handful of her plump rear, feeling my cock jump in my pants.

"Okay," she says, pushing away slightly. "Before this goes beyond the point of no return, what did you have to tell me?"

"Well…" I swallow, hard. All of the sudden I'm tripping over my own tongue. "It's not that I have something to, um, tell you so much…"

"Aww. Look at your cheeks turning all pink." Bridgid pinches my cheek until I yelp. "What's got you so nervous? I already said I'd wear the Princess Leia outfit; you just have to get off your ass and order it—"

"This isn't about that," I say hastily. "It's just…I don't have something to tell you so much as, um, something to ask you."

I fumble in my pocket and draw out the tiny velvet covered box within. As I sink to my knee, realization dawns in her lovely umber eyes. Bridgid's hands go over her mouth and a tiny squeal erupts from behind her fingers.

"Bridgid, will you marry me?"

"Hell yeah, I'm gonna marry you," she says, sticking out her finger so I can slip the ring into place. She barely glances as the rock before grabbing my necktie and using it to drag me to my feet. Then she mashes her mouth into mine, and we share a sublime moment of intimate connection.

Curiosity is all that makes me want to break away, albeit temporarily. I push her away slightly and cock an eyebrow.

"Thank you for saying yes, but what was it you wanted to tell me?"

Bridgid laughs softly. She traces a line across my chest with her painted nail.

"Well, I'm really glad I insisted you go first, that's for sure."

"Why is that?"

She smiles coyly. "Because I found something out, and I wasn't sure how you were going to take it. I still sort of don't, but..."

"What? Did Starbucks offer to buy out your bakery or something?"

"What? No!" She playfully punches me in the gut. "No, you big goof. This is what I found out."

She reaches behind her and takes something out of her back pocket. Bridgid holds the white plastic tube up to my eyes, where a recess displays a blue line.

"What's this?" I ask.

"You're going to be a daddy, that's what this is."

My eyes widen, and I sweep her into a bone-crushing embrace. I've never been so happy in my entire life.

Then I scoop up my bride-to-be in my arms and carry her upstairs to the bedroom. Dinner can wait.

I'm hungry for something else entirely.

———

I hope you enjoyed Bridgid and Joel's story! Looking for more from the Muffin Top Bakery series? Check out *Triple Bond*...

One-click Triple Bond Now!

Regina never thought she needed a man to be happy... then Michael came. Except, he didn't

make her smile with joy. No, he made her *furious*.

Sure, Regina has always been a bit stubborn and independent. That's what makes her such a good lawyer. But now she's in a bind because she has to resolve her mother's estate and, for the first time, she needs some help. She caves, puts her ego aside, and reluctantly asks for assistance…

And gets *Michael Pickett*.

Seriously? Did it have to be *him?* Sure, he's a brilliant attorney with a body to die for. And yeah, he definitely fills out a suit in the most delicious ways, but… he's the most stubborn and independent person she's ever met since…

She's looked in the mirror!

That's right. He's a male version of Regina—the two of them constantly at odds until they realize one simple thing:

Sure, they hate each other with a fiery burning passion.

But…

They might also love each other with that same intensity.

One-click Triple Bond Now!

Excerpt from Triple Bond

Regina

It's been a couple months since Mama's funeral, and I can't say it's gotten any easier with time. Things still haven't died down yet, which has begun to really take its toll on me. I spend every single day in Mama's office trying to sort through her finances.

Everything is such a mess; it took weeks just to even get everything organized enough, so I could really look at it. Trying to get her estate settled has proven to be the most challenging. I love Mama, but I really wish she hadn't left us such a mess. It angers me sometimes that she never called me before she got sick to come out here and help out.

I fought with Bridgid all the time in the beginning about how alone and overwhelmed I was feeling, but she's so consumed in her new marriage with Joel that I don't think she really even heard me. I don't blame her. Mama's death was the hardest on her, so I try not to bother her with much anymore.

I think losing Mama really showed all of us what is really important in life. I was never really close with any of my sisters, which was mostly my fault. But lately, Trulia and I have been spending so much time together bonding and really learning about each other for once. It feels good to finally be close with her, I just hate that Mama isn't here to see it.

If things weren't good between Trulia and I right now- I don't know what I'd do. She's been helping me deal with the fact that I got let go from my job right before Mama got sick. If it were any other job it wouldn't be hitting me this hard, but I had been working there for as long as I can remember. I dedicated so many years of my life to that place, not even allowing myself to have a social life because of it. I've never been in a situation like this and it's left me in a tailspin for sure. I'm still trying to get back on my feet.

Regardless of everything, I'm just really happy that I'm finally here with my sisters after so many years of being separated. I left Texas not long after I turned eighteen, and so did Trulia. Bridgid is the only one that stayed. Of course, Tru and I still visited for the holidays and such- but it just wasn't the same. It's been almost twenty years since the three of us were all living in the same place. We've got a lot of catching up to do- that's for sure.

It gives Tru and I something to bond over, the fact that we both moved away from home so soon. I think I always judged her for moving to New York City to be an artist. I always just assumed she was slacking off and not really making anything of herself. Turns out she's actually amazing at what she does, and she deserves a lot more credit than she gets.

It's funny because the two of us are so opposite. I've always been more high-strung, more controlling and demanding- I can admit that. Meanwhile, Trulia has always been the easy-going, calm, go-with-the-flow type. I think that's good though- we balance each other out.

I'm in Mama's office sorting through some papers when Tru calls to me that dinner is ready. Sighing, I shove everything aside and make my way to the dining room. This has become our routine. I spend the day going through all the files and such, while she sorts through Mama's belongings and packs things up. Then she gets sad looking at all of Mama's things and starts dinner. It's really very depressing.

Tonight's menu consists of tomato soup and cheesy garlic bread- which we have at least twice a week. We sit down across from each other and dig in.

"Do you know how to make anything else?" I complain.

"Hey, you're welcome to do the cooking for once if you so please," she rolls her eyes.

"Yeah I'm not Bridgid."

"Exactly," she smirks.

We sit in silence for a couple minutes, dipping our bread into the soup.

"So how's the estate coming?" Trulia breaks the silence.

"Honestly? I'm so fucking overwhelmed. I have no clue how things got so messed up. I really don't think I can sort everything out on my own. It's a disaster, Tru."

"I'm sorry… I wish I could help."

"Trust me, you are helping," I shoot her a smile. "Just being here with me is helping… I don't know what I'd do if you weren't here with me every day."

"Well good, I'm glad. Maybe Bridgid can offer some help?"

"I don't think we should bother her… she was the one here with Mama every day. I look at it like this is our payback for leaving. She deserves some time to just sit back and enjoy her life. Besides, I don't want to disrupt her and Joel's bubble."

"I understand. I'm sure she would appreciate you thinking of her. I try not to even mention what's going on over here during our weekly calls. I don't want to upset her."

"My how the tables have turned," I sigh.

Trulia nods, finishing up the rest of her soup.

"I have faith in you, Reggie. You're gonna get it all figured out, I know it."

I wish I believed in myself the way she does. Because right now I'm about ready to throw my hands up. I clean up the table while Tru does the dishes, and head back to Mama's office for another long night.

One-click Triple Bond Now!

About the Author

Hey readers! I'm Tasha Hart, author of contemporary romances. Thanks for reading my stories. From a young age, I've been inspired to tell stories about the ideas I have all the time. It started with telling wild stories, then some wilding of my own... but now I'm settling down with some good coffee and trying to write great books. It's a lot like running, which is what I usually do to figure out how my characters are going to misbehave. Totally distracting, consumes me wholly in the moment, and then it feels like magic! If you like reading my stories, consider pushing the Amazon follow button so you'll get notified when I've got a new book release!

Find Tasha online at… https://tashahart.com